MELVYN BRAGG

Melvyn Bragg is the author of fourteen novels, the most recent being the bestselling THE MAID OF BUTTERMERE, A TIME TO DANCE and CRYSTAL ROOMS. He also wrote the screenplay for the television dramatisation of A TIME TO DANCE. He has written several works of non-fiction including RICH: THE LIFE OF RICHARD BURTON, film screenplays and, most recently, a play entitled 'King Lear in New York' which opened in July 1992 at the Chichester Festival Theatre. He is editor and presenter of *The South Bank Show*, and Chairman of Border Television. Born in Wigton, Cumbria, Melvyn Bragg now lives in London and Cumbria.

Melvyn Bragg

THE NERVE

British Library C.I.P.

A CIP catalogue record is available from the British Library

ISBN 0-340-51854-5

Printed and bound in Great Britain for Hodder and Stoughton Paperbacks, a division of Hodder and Stoughton Ltd, Mill Road, Dunton Green, Sevenoaks, Kent TN13 2YA. (Editorial Office: 47 Bedford Square, London WC1B 3DP) by Clays Ltd, St Ives plc.

To
C.H

I

The nerve was worse and yet it was such a small complaint. It had twitched at the corner of my left eye for days. I knew almost nothing about illness and at first was pleased to imagine that it was caused by a bug— some minute and venomous germ looting and rampaging under my skin. Soon it became too irritating for such an elaboration and I settled on the nerve. My eye was half closed and wept. I had no idea what might salve it, nor was I used to going to the doctor for such an apparently minor ailment. I waited for it to go away.

On that Saturday morning, it seemed to attack me the moment I woke up. Possibly its stupid twitching alarmed me out of sleep. No dream chased me into consciousness; I'm rarely woken by dreams. If it weren't 'proved' that we all dreamed, I'd say I never dreamed. I was more likely to be disturbed into life by the dustcart which cleared the street on that, as every Saturday morning. It made a sound like an animal, a horse perhaps, but one which had been trapped and ironed by an engine, become half-beast, half-machine. Now the chained animal was forced to heave in its breath, uttering these terrible metallic groans while it fed on the rubbish of the streets, forced to suck in gutters where once there had been grass.

I was afraid of noise by then and tried to pacify these new London street cries by such fantasies.

After the dustcart had passed by I distinguished other sounds : wirelesses, next door downstairs and across the street; the high-heeled trot of the nurse in the flat

7

above; the intermittent revving of his motor-bike by the boy who spent all weekend stripping and reassembling it; the flapping of children's sandals as they ran along the pavement; and behind all that the ceaseless boom of cars from the main road, forty yards away. No aeroplanes though, thank God. But no milk float either—the clattering of the bottles was a cheerful noise, like the sound of the children, both reminders of a time when noise had been companionable. I lay still but for the twitching eye, trying to shore up the ruins of myself against another day.

Perhaps it is possible to imagine all this noise as music. If you cut it into suitable lengths it would be not unlike some contemporary compositions; such an urban assault had possibly inspired the composers in their work. But I like tunes and harmonies, birds and silences; none there, none here. Birds might still announce the dawn but forty-ton lorries and man-shaking drills enter and occupy the day.

It is difficult now, in this home, accurately to recapture that waking. Memory is not enough; what has happened since has discoloured it. But I think it is accurate to say that within a few moments of leaving sleep I felt in danger. My throat was sore and so constricted that I had to suck at the air as I'd imagined the dustcart sucking at the debris. Some unnameable fear lit a fuse along my veins and the blood spurted coarsely through my chest; heart hammering against the rib-cage as if it were balsa wood and rice paper. And in the centre of my mind, a violent exhaustion pleaded for more sleep, oblivion, an evasion of the day—a mercy which my body would not grant.

Getting up was an act of will and in the command I found some relief. Getting up was often an act of will for everyone. One of my most effective goads to action was to invoke 'everybody': it usefully diminished self-importance, found safety in the numbers. But such methods were losing their potency.

I drew the curtains. The first dare. I drew back the curtain to look out on this street I had come to live in nine months previously: a street which had accompanied the desperation and in many ways acted as a metaphor. On that morning I looked in such a way as someone might have peeped over sandbags at the Front. However inappropriate that comparison appears it is the truth of how I felt. The street was the outside world and what was outside me was against me. Moreover, that drawing apart of the curtains was a definite act: I emphasized this by accomplishing it in a manner which had just a slight air of theatricality. For, somehow, I felt that this oppressive, still subdued fear I was enduring made me a player where before I'd been one of the audience. I was the drama now, the play.

That small, self-important revelation was difficult to make. Once I would never have dreamt of allowing myself so to draw attention to myself. Even when alone. But by that time appearances were flaking off, the manner was no longer being nourished by the matter, the style of life I had constructed could no longer deal with the content. Now, writing this, I wonder at the past time before that day: a time of certainties in appearance and manner and style; even with regret at its death.

The room to which I turned had grown out of a regard for such certainties; a regard for the world and my place in it. It was to be seen as well as lived in: as if some god, a compound of mother, teacher, employer, heroes, revered men dead and alive, of fears and fantasies and infantile longings—as if this demanding monster sprawled across the ceiling knowing that the furniture was arranged for its gloating appraisal; or, more accurately, to appease it.

It was eighteen feet by fifteen and served as bedroom and sitting room: the bed, when covered with an

Arab blanket and littered with small cushions, became (I hoped) a settee. No one had ever sat on it. There had never been more than three people in the room and I had three armchairs—bought in junk shops like all my furniture, none costing more than a few pounds and each, I had once thought, 'stylish'. I had not cared what the style was as long as it was there: as long as it was as unlike my mother's careful Co-op cosiness as possible. The armchairs lounged around the room with a certain battered grace, I used to think, the commodities of a previous century grown to distinction with the years. There were oil paintings on the walls—portraits, eight pounds ten the lot. Intermixed (casually I'd say to myself), set against the 'old', were two works in cork and plywood by former students of mine—both painted white and very large—and various prints and sketches I'd picked up cheaply. There was a wardrobe, and of course a desk neatly stacked with my notes, a couple of well-worn Persian mats and knick-knacks from cultures and climates I'd never known. Most of all there were books—almost two thousand of them—covering two of the walls.

When I put on a side light in the evening and the street quietened down, then some reality was given to an adolescent dream of a book-lined study, scholarship, peace, learning—the daydreams of the swot I'd been. No need to list the books in detail: yards of hard-backed English classics, bought for sixpence each in their twentieth Victorian reprint; scores of Penguins; inches of European 'moderns'. Interspersed with these (which I saw as the 'backbone' like those few oil paintings) were books on religion and psychology, philosophy and sociology as well as lectures and old sermons and oddities: no pornography. Like the paintings on the wall, and the furniture, but much more personally and powerfully, those books represented a background I had made for myself. Neither of my parents could have

10

read one of them without falling asleep; nor could I, now.

I have spent some time describing that room because I spent a great deal of time in it. I could say more: talk of the way the position of the paintings had once pre-occupied me for days: recollect the circumstances of each purchase: try to transmit the excited feeling of having 'arrived' when first I'd sat alone in this womb of my making and self-consciously 'dipped into' a book. I'd deliberately chosen a heavy leather-bound volume—Middleton's Dictionary of the Arts. That moment had crystallized something: how soon the crystal had disintegrated.

I had a kitchen and a bathroom as well and had felt very sure of being snug when I'd taken the flat; even though the nurse from upstairs had to pass through my corridor, and the two men who lived below would sometimes site their quarrels in the downstairs passage. But the bathroom was a sanctuary. The habit, too, of bathing in the mornings had still not lost its strangeness although I'd begun it at university twelve years previously. I'm thirty.

I'd begun a new life there. A way of thinking about things as well as doing them : that is not clear enough. But all those who have been brought up in households where analysis is not brought to bear on any subject, where topics and people are discussed or dismissed according to custom or prejudice, will know what a revelation and what a strain it is suddenly to discover that there can be explorations and questions. And what a reaction, also, when, a few years later, you discover that there are no certain answers. Only in the past are there certain answers.

Usually, I'd open the taps and then stroll back into my bedroom—now become a sitting room with the laying on of the Arab blanket—and I'm sure I did this on that morning. I liked to stand by my desk in my dressing-gown, the water toppling into the bath, and

11

'glance at my notes'. I was a lecturer in General Studies at a north London technical college and was then preparing a new series of lectures on the Arts and Contemporary Society. Once I would have been eager to give you a précis of this but now it seems to hold as little interest as the furniture or the books. It is all part of a construction which became obsolete. Possibly it had been undermined for years or at least for months: but one day there was no more love for it. I still pretended, however, or did not recognize the lack, and on that morning would have 'leafed through' my notes and perhaps even remembered the pleasure I used to find in doing so.

I put on the kettle, a low flame, timed to coincide with the bath—it was a minor triumph to programme the operation precisely. Coffee, fruit juice, toast and cheese for breakfast—my mother would have considered it no start to the day: more; the cause of all my trouble.

While I am still hesitant about continuing this, let me give you a little more information. Besides the lecturing job, I also do book reviews for a quarterly magazine called *The Novel*. It has intellectual ambitions which it achieves, I think, and, coincidentally, its circulation is very limited. It pays no one a fee. I have occasionally reviewed for one of the 'heavy' Sundays—but never enjoyed it; the possibility that many people would see my name in print somehow made me uncertain of the value of anything I said.

My flat is in north London in Hampstead, near the Heath. It's strange and rather amusing that I should be in a district which attracts as many clichés as the one in which I'd been brought up. People in the Lake District —where I was born—were constantly being caricatured as 'Dalesmen', 'Slow-thinking but hard-headed', 'Shrewd countrymen' and so on; so many tourists *wanted* the people to be as unchanging and as easy to

12

identify as the Lakes themselves that there was even more of sloppy social anthropologizing than usual. Everyone who has lived in a rural area must know how useless it is to attempt to counteract the weight of this patronizing opinion: in the Lake District, a rural area which was also a beauty spot, the weight was sometimes oppressive. And at university—I went to Bristol—there was the cliché of the Northerner to be bored by: where he'd once been thought of as Blunt and Thrifty and Common he was now expected to be Bright and Abrasive and Original. This spurious North-South dialectic worked both ways because when I returned to the Lakes I was suspected of being Soft, Smooth and Southern. While Hampstead—one of the areas in London in which a number of writers, film people, teachers and painters live —Hampstead was supposed to be Intellectual, Arty and Smart. No mention would be made of the working people who made up the bulk of the population in the district.

For me it was ideal: near work, near a tube station, near shops and cafés and, most of all, near the Heath, open countryside on a miniature scale within half an hour of the centre of the City.

To risk a generalization—which I attempt to puncture or deride in the writing of others—this addiction to labelling is so pervasive that even English class snobbery cannot fully account for it. Probably it is something to do with tribalism—a wish to keep groups both small and quickly identifiable for easier co-habitation or more rapid extermination. I want a tribe. What is relevant to this account is that I was very aware of the cliché I had walked into so willingly and though I would not admit its accuracy to anyone else or *of* anyone else, nevertheless I used to think it *did* apply to me. That somehow I *was* Intellectual and Arty—and even (in consequence) Smart: and I then thought that I was secretly grateful to borrow such a definite personality from the district, having destroyed forevermore that inner source from which

13

springs a unique character. As I had in some way been ejected from my former mind by what I had read in books, so I was rejected by my former social place and found myself grasping at available clichés. Sometimes I would be amused to imagine that my mind had broken out as from a chrysalis (this was during a brief optimistic period) : but the wings were irreparably harmed and where could the poor butterfly lodge but under the nearest cabbage leaf ? Alas.

A final—probably unnecessary—addition to this antidramatic introduction : all the talk of 'my mind' and so on—do not think that I consider it to be special other than that it is my own. Its comparative failure on important occasions—in examinations and interviews and on many blank pages intended for fiction or verse—this failure was undoubtedly a cause of unhappiness and strain. Nor was it the failure of a mighty circuit which just happened to 'short': there was not enough power there in the first place.

Nevertheless, it would be useless for me to attempt to disguise the fact that for long periods of my life the inner landscape—conscious as well as unconscious—has been more absorbing than the outer. Dully staring over some inchoate reflection has been more to my taste than browsing through nature; sprinting through a book was more alluring than spinning around streets : thinking was more satisfying than doing. Fiction's more real to me, more affecting, than facts.

I have now taken you right out of that morning, those moments in the room on that day, and digressed perhaps too much. But even as I have been writing I have been doubting whether I could actually bring myself to put down what did happen. Once the first confession is made—why do I call it a 'confession' as if sin were involved in an act whose farthest causes might have been to do with the total failure of Christian faith ?—

once that event is described then I, as present narrator, can move back and let the story take over.

It is this first person, too, which causes anxiety. This 'I' who is such a former self, such a stranger, nearer fiction than fact.

In the bathroom, then—I made a point of opening the windows wide, already feeling a little stuffy on this warm August morning—I undressed and glanced at the mirror. The eye was swollen; seeing it so definitely out of order reassured me a little. My anxiety, that shiver of fear even, this swelling could be their valid cause. I tried not to look at my body: at school I'd gone through a period of sickening (secret) narcissism and even now it would break out if I encouraged it: like a rash just waiting for that first scratch to flare out in force. Though I wear glasses—affectedly, really: I only need them for reading—and in the past deliberately repressed natural open movement as being too vigorous and so too exhibitionist, thus making my physical appearance that of someone diffident and apologetic, I have the build of a farm labourer. It used to embarrass me. Hulking, proportioned for endurance, not grace— ugly and hairy. The determination (or the fear) which had once succeeded in forcing *that* form to imitate a notion of aesthetic langour is distressing.

In the bath I expected to relax. Instead, the water seemed to remind my skin of its vulnerability and immediately the veins and nerves, the blood and the pulse panicked. My body was shuddering as if a violent infection had just overcome the last resistance and was swarming under the skin plundering the integrity of everything it encountered. Then I felt I was bleeding, under the skin, that the blood had seeped out of the arteries and was streaming down my body, wave after wave down. And my head cramped, like a muscle it cramped. I pulled myself upright and got out of the bath. Stood still trying to turn the shivering into the acceptable shaking of a wet body in cool air: but the air was too warm to allow the excuse.

I tried to pretend to look for a cause for this; to listen for any loud noises, invoke unpleasant experiences which might relate; tried whatever I could to keep away this swarm from my head. I opened my jaw and yawned as widely as I could to loosen the grip of the cramp. Outside I heard the jostling of the milk bottles on the milk float: once, I had delivered milk, during a summer holiday from school—the picture of myself in short pants going up the garden paths on the council estate with a holder which carried four pint bottles slackened the cramp for a moment. Now I thought of this attack as being against an oppression— a counter-revolution; as if my body were rebelling against that part of myself which had once tyrannized it. I stood, wet, naked, leaning against the basin, hoping (crying out inside myself) that this would not also happen inside my head. The past; that would help, I thought: and, just before it came, I thought; the present, too. Don't go away, don't give up this day, don't collapse and be taken away—this day must be lived through because one life is murdering another; if inside you are slaughters and executions you must keep awake, keep in existence through it all or it will be only a dead body that is left.

It came. The walls of my mind crumbled and I imagined black blood seeping down the grey linings of my brain; penetrating that thinnest of membranes which keeps separate the complexities of a life. Blankness and silver screens which streaked to blankness once more. Like water now; like the sea it was beating down an old wall it had long made rotten. And now the entire brain slipped its moorings and was dashed around the skull which had become an ocean, and was thrown up on waves of ancient sickness which spewed from forgotten casks the storm had revealed and broken open:

16

there was no steering this mind—for now it was a bladder, a small discoloured bladder, which was slowly being sucked down into a swamp of vomit—and again it was blood and the walls flaked away, so thin they were, so fragile, to reveal blackness, blackness, no guide, no light. I had the past. I had the day. The milk float was passing by. The water would be boiling over. My eye was closed and when I touched the nerve, it was like fingering a detached knob of flesh. There was mucus coming from the eye now. I pushed myself from the basin and moved towards the kitchen: a kick in my throat forced me to stop. I felt I was swallowing a baby—very old, raw, unskinned, screaming. It was in my throat.

*　　*　　*　　*

'Bloody baby. Bloody kid. Bloody baby! Get in that kitchen. Get out of my bloody road. Won't lift a spade? Your father's got to lift a spade and more than a spade a bloody sight more. Can't do it because of your clothes? What kind of bloody talk is that? Your bloody mother shouldn't put you in clothes like that if you can't work in them, and don't look at that bloody book —look at *me*! Look at somebody that works for his living—with his hands—see—see that broken nail— want to know how I tore that? Put that bloody book DOWN. Bloody clean clothes! When did I last get a new jacket? When did she buy *me* a bloody new jacket last? Eh? Pour us a cup of tea. Now! You can do that in your school blazer, can't you? It's like bloody Irish stew anyway. It'll need a lily-white hand to stroke it through that spout. And don't set your face like that at ME. I'm your father even though your mother's trying to make you ashamed of it. Git!

'Sit on that chair. On THAT chair. Sit. Sit up. UP! Now. Now then. Now.

'We should be able to talk to each other. Eh? Ted? You talk enough to your mother. Bloody well talk to me.'

'I want to, father, I want to. Or, I'm frightened not to. But this sweat, all over me. I can't. And I'm watching your hands. Ready to dodge. I *wanted* to help you in the garden but my mother would kill me if I messed up my school things. She would. Say nothing—you know. Nothing but just *look*. And that would kill me. Whatever I did forevermore afterward would never make up for that. Why do you have to shout so much? How *can* I like you when you shout so much? You want me to do things with you—you say that—but only things that will get me into trouble with her.'

'I've been working on my own all day, my bloody lonesome, do you understand that? In those fields, cutting that dyke; not even a road next to me for cars to go past me and have a look at. I want to talk to somebody lad, eh? Have your*self* a cup of tea with me, eh? Before your mother comes back.'

'When you talk gently like that it's even worse. I can't answer then because of the lump in my throat. When I try to bring up a word, the lump seems to stamp on it, push it back into my body. It's painful, like those moments just before you cry.'

'Say *some*thing, lad. Neither of you have a word for me nowadays. Is it any wonder I shout? Is it any wonder I go out? The wonder is that I come back.'

'We don't want you to come back. Or, she doesn't. When *I* think of you never coming back I can't think any more. I can't imagine what might follow.'

'You stick in, lad. Don't take any notice of me. You stick in with your schoolwork and your books and doing what your mother tells you. I mean it—yes—listen. No, no—I'm not getting at you. You keep to it. You keep working. And *never* cross anybody, Edward: never cheat anybody: never get into any debt, and with the education you'll have by the time she's finished with you—you can't go wrong. Made for life, you'll be, after all that: set up for good.'

And later when I grew up and his threats became pathetic gestures, I would look at that exhausted man and beside the pity and the fear, have this question in my head. How could I follow him? If we grow by imitation; if we live by what we see and have imagined from that then how far could I travel in his steps? He who had been defeated after what could have appeared the first independent victory of new manhood—his marriage? I'd already 'passed' him at school, as easily as I had outgrown him in height. Now I look back through the confusion of tears and misery. Then, I could not bear him who should have borne me.

'You're a good lad. A good lad. You're a good lad to your mother. You *are*—though I say it myself—you're better than I was to mine. You are. And I'm sorry I said "bloody".'

*　　*　　*　　*

There's a stage of drunkenness where your only contact with consciousness is the feel of a solid object touched by your body. Or when you are in a fever and your hand touches the bed-clothes or encounters the bed-side table—the touch renews associations which had disappeared.

That's the nearest I can get by comparison with other experience to telling you how I survived the next few minutes. It was worse than either of those: much worse.

I remember leaning my face into the steam which surged from the kettle spout: I let it condense on my skin, perhaps hoping it would wash away the fear. And my hand, so heavy and numb, the clumsy hand. (I might have tried to make it appear comical; I used to do that as a trick for relief, later: *then* I'm sure I would still have been completely unnerved by the leaden thing which swung by my side and terminated in chunky, unfeeling fingers.) I reached for the security of the quilted oven glove and eventually lifted the kettle off the gas and even managed to knock off the gas: but I put the kettle down again. A cup would have had to be found, a saucer, a spoon, Nescafé, sugar, milk—it was all too difficult and exhausting. I could have cried at the labour involved and perhaps there were tears mixed with the substance which still dribbled from my bad eye.

How to staunch this wound inside my head? I went into the big room and sat in the chair which was angled to 'take in' the most imposing view of the books. Their titles seemed to peel off from the spines and dive into my brain; like midget planes; suicide pilots; titles crashing into the débris of my skull. Born the week war was declared: through childhood and adolescence a mind bombarded by images of machines and men at war and I saw that for the previous months my mind *had* been like a battleground; snipings and bombings, assaults and retreats, the language and the pictures suited the facts. And then that nerve helped detonate the big bomb inside my head and fear pushed out all else. I considered: no, not 'considered'. All this time the waves beat over me, each time threatening to drown me. I *wanted* to get up from that chair and dress. I knew how to do that.

But once more came that terrible sensation of the baby in my throat and once more the throat was constricted. The child grew into a monster—a scabby, festering, infected thing—made up of suppressions and surrenders, of aborted ambitions and miscarried attempts: it reached out to murder the life it should have had. On many nights the spools of thought had come off the brain's projector and I'd watched my life screened at crazy speeds in crazy order—but the comfort then had been in the obvious 'madness'; and the

20

explanation for that in the obvious strain. Scientific analogies—though only partly understood—were a help: like a circuit being overloaded, and so on. But this, this great heave of fear, this displacement as if the reality of a moon had dropped too near the ocean and sucked out the sea—this could not be thought of as something that might happen again: I might not be able to survive this first time. If only I could get out of the chair and get dressed: but between the desire and the decision was the gulf out of which were clambering these malignant destroyers. Once more there was some slight relief in animalizing the danger: better they were fiends, or distorted and crippled remainders of former selves—better that than they be unknown, unnameable. I wanted to be free to stand.

Voices from the street. Like boys taunting each other in the schoolyard—the National Primary School where I'd gone to, built in 1840, condemned in 1912, still used in 1950—its yards and high walls exactly like the prisons and workhouses and lunatic asylums of the period: the same period as my present street. Now, below, was the same ringing of shrill excited tones against high faces of brick.

Remembered: 'Go on then. *Start* it!' '*You* start it!' 'I've already started it!' 'Start it again.' 'Right ... I will.' 'Right then.' 'Right—there. There, I've started it.' 'Yes. You've started it now.' A Fight! A Scrap! A Fight! A Fight! Squeaking, shrill, they'd rush to the shores of the scrap and jostle for a view. 'Get him! Hit him! Get him!' Sickness in the gorge and sweat on the palms. Baying boys—sulky when too soon the schoolmaster came out to stop the messy contest.

That was the sound from the street and it drew me from the chair to the window where I stood and peered down, swaying as if the real blood were streaming from my head as rapidly as the imagined blood. But watching. Praying for the incident to conduct me through memory to present coherence.

* * * *

'You bloody try it, mate. *You*—bloody try it. Go on—go on—go on.'

It was no contest. The muscular young skinhead who drove the milk float would have murdered Mr Snell. Both of them knew it: and he was brave—bad-tempered middle-aged Mr Snell who lived in the basement flat with a 'wife and one and another on the way', and a Standard Ten for his front garden, a third-hand vehicle which received fanatical devotion—brave not to scuddle back down his basement steps as rapidly as he scurried up them whenever his Standard Ten was threatened.

'I'm just saying'—he found difficulty in just saying that: but he kept on. Perhaps the gathering crowd, the window-watchers and morning-shoppers—perhaps they were protection—'I'm just saying that you should be more careful.'

'WHAT DID I *DO*? Eh? I've seen your sort. You rabbitin' prick. WHAT DID I DO? Eh?'

'I'm just saying . . .' He repeated his previous low-pitched sentence.

I could imagine Mrs Snell alone in the back room of the basement—the bottom layer of our four-storeyed building—much younger than her husband. Too much. Even to an outsider like me the discrepancy obviously aggravated jealousy which a natural bad temper was frequently ready to act on: or it encouraged gestures which occasionally, as now, were shown to be gestures only.

'It's YOU,' said the young man, 'isn't it? Eh! It's YOU complains to the bloody council about the dust-bins in this street, isn't it? Don't tell *me*. I know them *all* on the lorry. I always knew it was you. Now I can tell. Eh. Come on then. Come on then. Show me where I scraped your bloody car then. Show me.'

The car was spotless, burnished rather than polished.

'I'm just saying . . . you have to be very careful with that float. It's a difficult thing to drive. Must be. Isn't it?'

'Don't try to suck *me* up! Show us that mark, mate, or I'll put one on you.'

But the threat was just that fraction less convincing: the instant having passed, the young man was finding it difficult to hold on to his anger and the justification for violence. The number of people now watching seemed to make him a little shy: he tried to enjoy his part as the innocent who'd turned on the bully—but his own reaction itself had so quickly turned to bullying that he was confused. He had no other tone, it seemed, for the situation: and the meekness of Mr Snell's manner now matching the comparative weakness of his appearance, the young man's threats became more strident, more in search of an enemy than confronted by one.

'I'm not looking for trouble . . .' Snell began.

'But you DID!' The youth was triumphant and momentarily revived. 'That's just what you DID! You came looking for trouble. Well you've *got* it, see.' He took two steps forward and prodded Snell on the chest. The older man, his hands in his pockets, rocked on his feet as if they were stuck in a rubber ball: and all expression fled from his face. He neutralized himself as far as is possible. Baffled, the youth turned and just before walking away, viciously kicked at the car's gleaming mud-guard.

'Bastard!' he said. 'Rotten bastard.'

He walked down to the milk float, accompanied by the horns from about a dozen cars now held up at different ends of the street by the float's inert occupation of the middle of the car-lined road. 'All right! All bloody right: ALL RIGHT!' He shouted—and the shouting appeared to cheer him up. He was grinning

23

when he started up the float and backed it into a parking space, bottles jostling, a cheerful sound.

Mr Snell watched all this with an expression most strenuously composed into thoughtfulness. His lips were pursed as if he were whistling absent-mindedly. *The Dam Busters* was his favourite tune. Once the youth was safely on the milk float he crouched, hands still in pockets, to look closely at the mudguard. Then, even more thoughtfully, he stood up, looked left and right and turned to 'amble' down the steps into his flat. I saw the white parting line in his hair, which was stiffly combed, military.

* * * *

Even at the time I probably *told* that incident to myself as well as watching it. Would fill out what I could not see : invent what I did not as a fact know. Perhaps to control it the more safely and so subdue it, or for the comfort of completeness. Or possibly as an instinctive hope of imitation. For if I could appreciate how others managed to move through the day, and could imagine that they *did*—then I, too, might survive.

* * * *

And I wanted to write it down. I remember that clearly. It began then. It was a form of reassurance—or revenge—or perhaps evidence of love for others, of an ultimate altruism. I kept saying—yes, I'll endure it, I'll let it come—because then I'll be able to put it down accurately. Throughout the day, whenever the images of breakdown, blankness, death and disconnection occurred there was this penultimate thought : At least let me survive long enough to write it down, to chart it, record it, to tell those who are there or have been there that another too has been 'pitched past

24

pitch of grief: no worst, there is none.' Others have witnessed—here's my mark.

Reconstructing and remembering it means I re-live it to some degree. . . . It can only be written in the interludes of strength or peace.

*　　*　　*　　*

After Mr Snell had gone inside I watched the street unknot itself and the traffic of cars and shoppers, of children and youths, reassert its pattern. Many people used our road as a short cut from the High Street to the Heath and the contrast between the elegantly costumed young people strolling down to the open space, and the tightly buttoned old ladies stiffly walking up for the scrounge of shopping in a crowded supermarket, was one of the contrasts in which I had once picked out city patterns.

Still then it was objects which filled my mind. That quarrel in the street had been to me as voices to a man in a black cell: the sounds were what had filled my mind, the rest I have added for this record. The voices were as objects, for, chiefly in that first half-hour—and how *long* it seemed: how long it *has* seemed since that day; most of my life has been experienced since then—that time was a time of objects.

The window pane which pressed coldly against my hand: pressed hard against it and finally pushed it away. The sun came through and printed heat on my face. I could feel the water gathering under the skin, the damp preparation in the pores and the heat penetrating my forehead and warming the disturbed greyness. My eye flickered: larger now, as if a tiny, violent bat were trapped between the lids and panicking.

I sat on the settee so lately a bed and the awkwardness of the posture . . . the thighs' underside pressed on the yielding mattress, skin being pulled by the towelled dressing-gown. . . .

I dared not go back in the bath, still full.

My clothes were two yards away. It would mean standing once more—comical now, it seems, the effort required for that: not then—and there would be steps to take; then the undressing and the dressing. The commonplace series of actions seemed to be beyond my capacity. Physically I was feeble in a strange way: I could not believe that my muscles would actually work —or, to be more accurate, I could not believe that anything I told them to do would have the least influence. Insofar as they did still drag through their duties it seemed to me because of the last whispers of memory: soon the commands would be heard no more and I have no power to issue new ones, they no more faith in the old ones. It was like moving jelly-like through jelly. Though I had managed to get from bathroom to kitchen to sitting room I'd been all the time conscious of phrases from boxing commentaries: 'groggy at the knees', 'sagging now', 'legs turning to water' and perhaps in some way I was punch-drunk or comatose: now even that jargon left me.

I still could not stand.

The sun was on my face again and I was sweating. I could feel it trickling under my arms, and—I hate the word—'crotch'. My skin prickled with sweat, as if the dirt were taking advantage of the sweat's outpouring to squeeze itself out of the skin; everywhere emerging, like a rash, like a secret infection swarming out. The sun was very hot on my face. I thought that it might ease the eye a little and turned to bathe the more in its rays.

The windows were dirty. I'd meant to clean them but it entailed climbing out and standing on a safe but narrow ledge: and I'd become timid about heights. More afraid of what I'd be tempted to do than of what might happen accidentally. I could see on the other

26

side of the street the plump woman in her white slip passing between her two windows as always. The sight upset me. The movement made her seem so caged, and that white slip was such a desperate promise; every weekend, Saturday and Sunday. I'd never seen her in the street itself.

Below, I could hear the children playing 'Catch and Kiss'. It was the little Indian girl who used to organize these games: she wanted to be kissed by Tim, a thoroughly English Boy with liberal parents and long blond hair. I used to watch them.

How *did* you move? How did I last move? Maybe the way was to have an objective. To decide that something worth having was not near and so had to be reached for. The amoeba's jelly parting its lips to reach for the particle which made it live.

What particle here?

Self-Reliance, Inner Resources, a grip on yourself. Take yourself in hand.

There were moments of less pain and less confusion and in those moments I felt peaceful at first. Then I learned to suspect and finally to dread them. They were the times you were revived in order to be beaten further. Even peace was no friend.

The ceiling started to tremble as Wendy started dancing. The volume went up and I heard a sound very near that of the old rock and roll groups which were popular when I was at school. Whenever one of these came on she started to dance—stomp would be more the word—a vehement reaction to the music.

Wendy's nursing had encouraged her to a breezy lewdness about sex. She thought I was a virgin and treated me accordingly. I could not quite understand why I not only accepted this but was relieved to play the part. It excused me from being myself, of course; but she was attractive and occasionally I regretted it. Her attitude, however, was set. Happily cut out for

27

caricature herself, she loved others to be just as simple to recognize.

The reverberations went through ceiling and walls to the floor where they affected a small table I had. One of its legs was just slightly short anyway: I stretched it with a wad of paper. A rather delicate early Victorian table on which I'd placed one of my favourite things—a piece of Roman glass, a phial for tears, beautifully shaped in that green lustrous glass. It began to shudder at the impact of the nurse's self-communing satisfaction. I got up to steady it.

Then, the whirlwind must have subsided for I must have dressed. I have no memory of this—nor of how I got out and onto the High Street.

* * * *

My mother comes to see me twice a week.

It's a difficult journey for her—two changes of bus, one entailing a wait of half an hour. The word 'entailing' is one I rarely use but in connection with my mother it comes naturally. I won't point out more things like that: this must not be a case history. I've read some of those, and they are not complete enough: they are not complicated enough; they are not frightening enough, or maybe they are but I gain confidence to write this by running them down . . . I used to get my confidence by building things up: by making them appear so difficult and so impossible that only the most superhuman efforts could lead to success: which would lead me to attempt superhuman efforts which did, of course, lead to a sort of success: in my mother's eyes at any rate. But this is fiction. 'I cannot paint what then I was' because it seems so long ago and my identity has altered beyond mere alter egos. I must invent what I was: as I must remember what I am.

My mother, then, comes here to this home where I

write this (and the planes sail over! Yes, here in 'the heart of the English Countryside'—the home used to be stately and a tourist attraction—even here the jets pass by, whining complaint), comes twice a week which is very good of her. She was always very good. She is unquestionably and unanswerably GOOD. A GOOD WOMAN.

My mother comes twice a week.

I'll waste no time on this place. I'm a voluntary patient. I have my own room—a neat and bare little cell, furnished as economically as a prison cell which suits me fine. The doctors come and talk—one in particular. I like the grounds and enjoy walking in them. Now that I'm almost better, I spend my time as industriously as a novice in a monastery. I rise, I read, I recreate.

When my mother comes I'm ready for her.

We are all supposed to be curious about sex in our generation. We are thought of as being licensed to enjoy all that was prohibited for parents and grandparents: those older like to imagine that we sprawl in lust and seize by day and night what they only dared in dreams and fantasies. But I never got what I wanted. By the time I had hairs and a man-size ... *why* is it so difficult to write the word? Why? Who am I afraid to offend? Do I ask out of fear or out of good manners? But oughtn't I to *hate* Good Manners? Aren't they part of a society which has repressed ordinary people and projected as virtues qualities which lead to mortal and spiritual violence? Somewhere still, inside me, as inside everyone, is that 'sound' of myself, against which I ring falsely or truly. How lost I am when I can no longer hear it—as for years I could not because I neglected to, preferring instead to be guided by 'standards' I thought I'd learnt from the books I'd read and the way of life I'd adopted, which said 'no' to impulse, at first sanely, sifting stupid from sensible, and then—by some extension of dimension (perhaps this new 'way of life' was afraid

29

and needed to consolidate its empire by extending its boundaries)—'no' was soon said to *all* impulses. *That* will teach my past, I seemed to be saying.

My mother would be upset to hear a four-letter word. And while I have sworn heavily at times, it has not been at times of hope. Yet I wonder how far her upset is feigned. She is still an attractive woman: as a girl, she must have been a honeypot. Even now, when she comes, there's always some nurse says, 'Your mother? She's too young to be your mother!'

I was writing about my sex life.

The fact is, I think, that by adolescence I was so titillated by expectations from inside and out, so inflamed by the subtle pornography of advertising, the reports and rumours of freedom and perversions, and all the cock-teasing of the modern world, that I was fit to bust. Put on the lid of a mother's puritanism, real or feigned it makes no matter: jam that cover on that geyser and there is only one way to hold it, and that is to bless it and seal it with the unction of maternal love. Unc. Unc. Unc-tion.

Irreproachable, unfathomable, and punctual twice a week she comes. Without fail.

To get what I desired? Me? In Cumberland? Then? Oh yes, a sniff, a hint, a touch, a peep at that divine mystery which would yet slither in the delight of its own vulgarity. Oh! Silk knickers and the godhead! Black suspender belts and the Life Everlasting! But to achieve the contemporary dream—me? Then?

NO. NO. NO. NO. NO.

I had a steady girl the last year at school (when I'd already got into University but was 'staying on' to 'read'). She was well padded against the cold that winter, in a massive woollen coat fit for a Sherpa or an Eskimo squaw come south on a trip. Ah yes. Now I can smile. But then, walking along the High Street, arm-in-arm, coat sleeve wadded against coat sleeve; or kissing—

spectacles to spectacles, misting up together; or trying to find a route through the buttons and battledress to that flesh which must exist, which would (I prayed) both flail and appease the lump which was like a steel shaft from my bowels to my throat—Oh, there were no smiles then. Look, you beautiful people: look around at the plain ones: see how they flinch into further plainness: see how they retreat before the billboards and centre-page spreads which call only for sylphs and satyrs, elegant and sensual, and imagine me, then, walking up the empty streets and down again, with the pressure of that heavily-coated arm on mine: in my head the furies and the limbs, the orgies and the ceaseless lusts of Sodom and Gomorrah: and by my side a very well brought-up girl who stopped me at the stocking top and slyly chatted about mortgages.

How do we survive?

I am no virgin but I have never spent the night I want to spend with a woman who loves me as I do her. Who will be as tender as I am and as bawdy as I am: who will take me as I would take her—completely, unquestioningly, shyly and greedily. *Never.*

You know the rest of it if you've read this far. I was not one of 'the beautiful people'. I wore sensible trousers and a sports jacket at university with a shirt perhaps coloured and in summer open at the neck. There were serious girls reading sociology and one painful confrontation with a Welsh whore after England had played Wales at Cardiff Arms Park and a group of us had gone to cheer. Why did I write 'whore?' I *liked* her, but it was so bloody horrible to mate for a pound with a girl so destitute.

I have come a long way from my mother.

But let me bring this unlovely catalogue up to date. I am as determined now that you shall know as once I would have been determined that you should not. Not because it is of primary importance: but it is certainly of sufficient importance and anyway it keeps me from confronting the three subjects I dread.

1. My mother.
2. The mother of my child.
3. That Saturday.

'Dread.' I have just looked up the word in the Chambers Twentieth Century Dictionary which was my prize for English Language, form 5A; July 1955. 'Dread (dred) n. great fear; awe; an object of fear or awe; (Spens) fury.' Then they go on to adjectives and transitive verbs and dreadnoughts and penny dreadfuls. This dictionary is one of the six books I allow myself here.

The last of my 'women-of-the-winter-coats' left me just before I moved into that Hampstead flat, so that by the time that Saturday came I, who was brought up with close female attention, had been without daily companionship for nine months or more. For, of course, age had taken me past the stocking-tops and I had lived with the last woman for a year. It is unfair to categorize them all by that thick 'winter-coat' and make all of them similar but then it is no more than the injustice which is the inevitable accompaniment of brevity and disappointment. None of them slid through into the internal dream which still went on, and with none could I feel satisfied and satiated: always there was failure, and often, of course incompetent, melancholy, dismal couplings.

They were good women, all of them : kindly sensible, careful, thoughtful, steady. Gone.

I took two of them home to meet my mother. She liked both of them. Neither, she said, would let me down. When she comes to see me, she always tries to steer the conversation towards one of them. . . .

Out! Out! Out with it! Now.

There *was* one. She came from the 'rough' end of the town and she was seventeen. I was feeling confident—

more than ever before or since in my life—full of confidence on that first Christmas vacation from university where I'd survived alone and steered myself through hurricanes of home-sickness. And suffered. So the return made me feel entitled to play the conqueror and in my new university tie I went to dances and there met Lizzie who worked in the jam factory and was flattered. Later I found out that she'd just been thrown over by her boyfriend—a buck as handsome as she, those days, was lovely as a roe. I'd never had my arms around anyone so beautiful, who trembled with wants and chatter and was restless and cheeky; now nuzzling, now tensing; now gazing at another man; now sucking my lips and sliding her hands up my body, as if she would strip my flesh. My mind and feelings *were* stripped and I went back to university at the end of that vacation near to tears. I had seen her daily and been clandestine. Never had I been so intoxicated and so secretive. I bought her clothes. At her insistence I left off my spectacles. I let my hair grow. I didn't look so bad then and even my mother commented that I was 'quite good-looking, really!' Of course I was confused about Lizzie. She prattled about pop-stars with such consuming conviction as made me jealous of them and bored by her. And what future *could* there be? Oh, fool, foolish man back there; you really *did* think that, didn't you? You sat and calculated it, even when she had just left you and your skin was alight and you were nearer than ever in your life to matching dreams and reality, for she made love like a tender girl who'd been injected all at once by a woman's lust and had only a little shame. Perhaps that is where your dream of sensuality comes from and it did not exist before Lizzie made it possible.

I left. I wrote. I received two replies and persuaded myself that no more could be expected. My memory of that second term is of a desert. The oasis I had drunk at became a constant mirage. I was always erect. I thought of her every second beat of the heart. When I returned to the town she was married. And two years later I found out that it was because she had been pregnant with my child. She hadn't wanted to 'bother' me.

*　　*　　*　　*

'You see, doctor, what I want to emphasize is that I'm as "average" as can be. Oh, I'm bright enough. But I'm average height, average weight, I have average tastes—or did have before I was afflicted with an education. Well let's use the word "normal". I've got normal desires and normal fantasies and normal needs and normal expectations, except that now my expectations have been refined and extended by the education I've received. So let's say "ordinary". I look ordinary. I speak in an ordinary manner and I act, my actions, my gestures—they're without frills or affection. I've had an ordinary life—except for that passage to intellect and the crisis which came from the resulting clash between body and mind, sex and will, roots and ambition, hope and desperation. That middle passage to a new world.

'What I mean is that I've always obeyed the rules. That's average and normal and ordinary, isn't it? I've looked both ways before crossing the street *and* looked right again : I never smoked downstairs in double-decker buses and where it said SPITTING IS PROHIBITED I did not spit. I brush my teeth twice a day: I use my vote : I pay water rates, council rates, electricity bills, gas bills, telephone bills, insurances, subscriptions and all my dues without fail. I don't assault people and if the man says ORDER PLEASE I say YES, thank you. When my students demanded that the system be changed I agreed with some of the demands and not with others and—like everybody else in the end—obeyed the resulting compromise. The landlord says: 'Time Gentlemen, Please'—and I drink up. I have worked hard. I have not been demanding. I have been a pagan, then an evangelist, then a Christian, then C. of E., then an agnostic, then an atheist, then a don't know, don't care, though I do! What more can I say? I have always done my bit and my best by the rules and regulations of this country which I like and the few people whom I love. I have done what I ought to have done

'And where I should have grown with the health of it all, being so willing to fit in, being so eager to please, I collapsed like a punctured lung.

'That is why I'm telling this story, doctor. I want them to understand—I want *you* to understand the hollowness of obedience. And *I* want to understand why that Saturday came and how it passed and where it has gone.'

Sometimes I pretend a doctor is there. Then I deliver monologues out loud. Afterwards I try to remember them and set them down.

That Saturday: I'm still running away from that Saturday. Every day helps: one day further. But it's nearer I want to be: for if I don't go out and meet it, I'll never know it. I must dare it again. In this writing.

2

One or two people glanced at me and I sweated: perhaps what had happened inside my head had in some way transfigured my face. I'd not had the courage to look at myself since dressing and leaving the house. I would see someone (I knew this) and there would be no connection between what was in front of my eyes and what was in my head. None. Just the space between.

But it was the lumpy, streaming eye which caught attention. For a while, it gave me some relief: it became an undeniable focus, and I fingered it as you might finger a lucky penny. Strange how that which was painful could also relieve pain.

Again and again in this account, this story, I run away into description. Yet how else can I put you where I was? Simply to hammer into your eyes the information that my mind was under ceaseless attack? Even were I to concoct similes so striking they would give off a thousand illuminations and recognitions that would only be part of it. 'We are in the world but not of it'; yet nothing enters the mind except by way of the senses: they lead to what is inside but are directed to what is outside. Of course, 'experience is itself a species of knowledge which involves understanding', and everything that reaches consciousness is already interpreted, already patterned. Nevertheless no one is outside the world and if half this story is about what happened inside my mind and the other half about the contingent coincidences and facts and indifferences of the world, then the proportion will not be ill-balanced.

36

Besides which, I am unable to give you the content in any other form. Some novelists, particularly the French, and especially the Franco-Irish Samuel Beckett, can so seal off a system that you sit inside the padded skull and watch the tock-tock-tock-tock of the quiet, tired, dispirited band which trudges in time to the cerebral clock. Perhaps the talk of 'the senses' and the invocation to empiricism is an excuse only. But I think not. Even on that day; even at the worst of moments; even when the bone of my head expanded and became a large dark cave full of terrors as real as those which threatened mythical adventurers in fairy stories; even when I felt the air become solid and my jaws having to work their way through it—even then, I saw and smelt and heard and tasted and touched: touched that agitated nerve and licked the two fingers that touched it, spreading my own ointment carefully on the whorled finger pads.

I also carried a book. I always carried a book. It was a talisman, a shield and a companion. I don't remember the title of that day's book. It would help me to invent one because I am sure that I related the few lines I read to the condition in which I found myself. When you are in an extreme condition everything relates: everything becomes both more clearly itself and more resonant with associations. What I *do* remember is that I could only read a few lines and then the print seemed to stick to the cells of my brain and be broken up by its heaving: the printed words seemed to excite yet more alarm. Perhaps it was the fact of having to think; perhaps it was that straw on the camel's back, that last thin layer of information which was unbearable.

Sometimes when I look back, I think that my breakdown—like many of a similar kind—was to do with the newness of things and the impact of change. So rarely, in a modern city, can your senses or your mind have any rest. And at school and university our minds were constructed to be curious. London feeds, even bloats, curiosity to bursting My own sense of privilege and luck, the knowledge which never left me that through my education I was being given a chance of lifetimes; this was a dynamo to the machine which the system had made ready for me to climb into. To vary the metaphor, we were trained liked thoroughbreds in those stables of learning—and then, most of us, turned out to do heavy work: but we could never forget the speed, the spring. The city's stimulation can glut an open mind, as it can make partly blind an open eye, and half-deafen an ear. We cannot be ourselves to the full because there is too much for us. Yet to be less is to be less of ourselves. When you are in a state of nervous upheaval, then you *are* claiming all of yourself for yourself: you need it: you *are* trying to be all of yourself all of the time—and the result is the avalanche.

I talk of breakdown: more often I think of it as a break*through*. I'd rather forget the word altogether: it comes from altogether too mechanical a view of a man. Cars break down; aeroplanes break down; rockets break down. People are nearer, say snakes, which change skins. Perhaps we change the skin of our being: and, because we are neither gods nor animals nor computers, because we are between, we are often caught half in, half out: or find no new skin grown; or discover the new skin to be so sensitive that it cannot tolerate the conditions it must meet. I had been living in part of myself and needed to reach out for the whole.

I have read about the workings of people's minds. Some of Freud and Jung and Adler: of the present-day writers Laing and Winnicott and Melanie Klein. Novelists have given more insights for me—Proust and Lawrence and Tolstoy: and poets and thinkers—I could fill lines with names so well known to a few that mention of them would be tedious or modish: so unknown to so many that they would be merely letters of the alphabet arranged as proper names. What I am saying about myself is to do with what I have found out by thinking about what happened to my self. It is hard to ignore what has been made of you. But any of you can test my experience against your own if you try to think how you think. Freud gave us a vocabulary for the unconscious: but that, though useful is unprovable. Perhaps we need a new vocabulary for consciousness; perhaps that is the renaissance we wait for now.

'Humankind cannot bear very much reality.' More a proverb than a line of verse.

I am happier with this small change of any educated man's mind than the strenuous business of that Saturday: that High Street: now I come round the corner of my own street and I am on it: the *noise*!

It was as if my skull enlarged itself, swelled up on my shoulders and laid itself across the road as across an executioner's block. And through it went the lorries full of rubble, grinding gears and whining brakes, the sports cars and motor-bikes, the 268 bus and the dustcart now proceeding on their business in this High Street at the busiest time of the morning: all drove right through that shell of skull.

I wanted to go back home. But was even more afraid of that. I had some shopping to do. There was a girl coming to tea. I was going to buy a cake.

On a Sunday morning, without the traffic, Hampstead High Street and Heath Street are lovely: Georgian shops, delicate shades of brick, alleyways full of galleries and antiques, pottery and bright goods: dozens of pubs and restaurants; bookshops, and eccentric clothes shops, delicatessens, launderettes, record shops, luxury shops: Victorian frontages—the hangover of a more stolid time—hardware shops, wood shops, old grocery shops and sweet shops, a cobbler, a fish and chip place and the most old-fashioned Woolworths in England; newsagents where they'd take ten minutes to get you the *exact* size of brown envelope, fruit shops where they'd rummage for the *best* apples; builders' merchants up some of those back alleys and, being Hampstead, all sorts of cottage industries in pretty backyards—furniture, mats, health foods, hand-painted posters, ties, shirts—within a few hilly acres was concentrated the variety of a huge city: those two streets were in some measure the quintessence of the West End of London *and* a lively suburb *and* a county town *and* a university area: and the alleys and slits between the walls, the unexpected squares and groups of trees and sudden revelation of Georgian cottages or Regency houses or Victorian strength or Edwardian grace—all this had made Hampstead seem to me to be the centre of everything I wanted from a *place* for a few years. That was when I'd come: and why I'd come.

I write this at a more hopeful time. Yet if you do not know the attraction the place once had—and so how powerful it was as a metaphor for a way of life—then you will not understand the effect of the dislocation I felt on that Saturday morning when I stood at the corner of my street, between the cigarette shop and the post-box and could see no connection between the substance which contained me and that which was outside me. This is why I write at such length about the place itself : for distance has now made a true dislocation and I must draw myself back there.

Like tinsel on a Christmas tree, like all the baubles and lights that wink and twinkle in the dark green branches, themselves every bit as attractive and confident and striking as the places were the people. It seemed they dressed for parts they claimed in the pageant of keeping the streets as decorative and interesting as their reputation, even as the caricature of their reputation demanded. And again it was a parade, in a small space, of what appeared to me examples of the more extravagant, perhaps more ridiculous, but certainly more decorative, aspects of English street dress of that time. The bewildering thing was that this aspect of 'fancy dress' seemed to affect everyone: so that old ladies, for example, whose poverty was, or ought to have been, apparent in ancient black ankle-length coats and hats of faded velvet, appeared almost as 'chic' as they did poor: like the old working-class 'characters' in those realms of patronizing middle-class English Literature.

The pavements belonged chiefly to young people and to that layer of the liberal middle-classes which conserves its youthfulness. The larger proportion of Hampstead's working-class population shopped at other centres within the borough. So there were beautiful legs, achingly long yards of thigh striding out of minuscule skirts which only needed a brush of the palm to slip them up to the waist: and the newer, long dresses which only a few were wearing in the heat and even here they took care to have buttons up the side, and even greater care to unbutton the buttons to way above the knee. Boys with long hair and medallions and rainbow-coloured jeans, immaculate actors, many people in scrupulous 'casual' wear; children dressed like hippie braves and hippies dressed like Indian squaws, and housewives dressed like teenage boys and teenage boys like teenage girls and teenage girls like objects of art—themselves the subject—and a collage of vivid materials laid on them with the care of brush strokes. If only I had been born ten years later! In my outfit—how conscious that street made me feel of appearance—in my quiet sensible clothes, *I* was a caricature too: 'Left-wing,' they would say (though I'd lost most of my interest in party politics by then), 'some sort of intellectual.' I was heir to the English upper middle-class tradition of plain living and high thinking; of Professor Joad taking strenuous holidays in the Lake District and saying, 'It all depends what you *mean* by "strenuous",' of the Brains Trust on the BBC and bread and cheddar cheese for 'lunch', of awkward thighs and baggy pockets, quirky hobbies and myopic attitudes—that stifling mantle had been held out for some of us who'd come in out of the dark and, foolishly, we had rushed to pull it on.

I stray around: no matter. One of the things I miss about modern novels is such straying: just this effect of rambling: a walk along a path which has time to stop and look over the gate at the hills, examine a wild flower, visit the old man on the hill, sit and smoke a cigarette behind a hedge. Besides which, in such a method there is a place for odd juxtapositions— not necessarily violent or symbolic or even obviously significant: merely those correlations which occur in everyone's life between one thing and another so that at the time of bust-up with a girl, for example, you can seriously have part of your mind engaged on whether or not you will take away with you the picture you bought together—but which *you* paid for and *you* like even though it hangs now in her room and meanwhile your life is wrenched out of your hands. Moreover, I *am* recreating that day, this story, and I want to comment on it by digression and description and so it helps to tell you that I am here now, writing in this room of eggshell-blue walls, this small room, silent and monastic, where my pen makes clearly audible sounds on these long sheets of lined paper given me by the registrar.

That is why I have taken so much space to describe Hampstead and even in that space described it so sketchily, saying nothing of the Churches, the Christian Science Reading Room, autumn wood-smoke in the lanes, the Brownies and the Buddhists, the flower-sellers, the leafy hinterland of rich suburbs where houses change owners for fifty/sixty/seventy thousand pounds, the great laboratory and the exquisite Regency Catholic church, for perhaps at that time I was only what I saw.

I have not the advantage of film or photographs—other advantages there are in writing—but the sense of a location cannot be dismissed. If by now you feel you know a little of that small hill overlooking the whole of London, flying in that August with all colours of clothes and displays and the gaudy overspill from the fair on the Heath—if you can imagine that place, skirted by areas of lesser cohesion and privilege, inhabited by all nationalities, with the Heath, like the massive grounds of ten thousand private houses—a place riddled with bed-sitters and small flats and claiming the highest suicide rate in England—here—you can see then why I came: why I left a contented suburb and the safety net of five years' acquaintances: why I wanted to pitch myself into it: and better understand the confusion when at first gradually and then relentlessly and finally, on that day, emphatically, the whole of this twentieth-century paradise of mine, this hillock of Xanadu, was thrown back into my face as I stood on the corner with a book, my head hurt by traffic, afraid to go on, afraid to go back.

I could have mentioned the place not at all. Made nothing of it. Described simply what I did and what happened to me. And perhaps, that place as a particular spot has not *so* much importance. But then the story would have had an abstract setting: been like this Home—nowhere: like this Home—anywhere: like this Home where my mother comes twice a week punctually to see me.

I think, rather, that she comes for *me* to see her. She is dying. She does not think I know: or if she suspects it she has not yet admitted it to her thoughts to any degree which allows it to be betrayed in her expression or in her actions, certainly not in anything she says. But she is dying: I sensed it and asked the doctor and pressed him until he confirmed it. She had told him so that he should 'know': she has not told me because she does not want me to be 'bothered'. I keep her secret.

She comes for me to see her to prepare for that time, soon, when I shall see her no more.

*   *   *   *

I moved because I was being watched. I like London because of the anonymity it offers. There is rarely a passing recognition: and if one does threaten there is always plenty of 'cover'. It allows great areas for harmless daydreaming, for playing the detective—particularly for that—or the criminal on the run: hunter and hunted coexist in the crowd in the city. You can send up flares of desire every minute, knowing they will be extinguished as quickly as any squib but seeing in those moments a possibility which has a real presence. The other side to the story of being bombarded in the city is this royal feeling of potent anonymity. But I was most definitely being watched.

The look reminded me of those glares which the young 'hard men', the Teddy Boys, used to throw at one another and occasionally at me at the dances to which I took Lizzie. She married just such a hard man. The glance said, 'Look back and I'll pick a fight: go on! Stare back and there'll be a murder.' He wore a dark suit, a white shirt, brightly white, opened at the neck, the collar carefully tucked over the jacket collar. As old fashioned as I was, in his way. A pale, tense, skin: black hair greasy and long, shaped by means of grease: a working-class man, probably a manual labourer judging from the strength in him and the roughness and size of his hands.

His intensity was like an emotional spear in the side of my mind. Silently I howled with fear and moved up the street. Mistaken identity? It must be, I thought, but was not reassured by that explanation for I remembered seeing him before: but I could not remember when or where.

As I moved, my Self seemed to be shredded by that noise and density of people and things, sights and presences: seemed to trail from me and stream out behind me. I wondered I did not shout out. My eye, fearing more hurt perhaps, was now effectively closed.

There was a pain in my chest. Where I thought the heart was. A fierce, sharp pain: as if a long darning needle were being pushed into it. I remembered the long pink darning needles used by my mother's mother clicking quickly in her mittened hands: she died before I started school. But surely that comparison is again inappropriate. A real needle sinking through skin and flesh and ribs into the heaving blood-pulse—that would be an intolerable pain, would it not? But so was this. Can I convince you merely by telling? For I *did* scream: but inside, inside that cavity of skull and the scream winged around it chased by its own echo which grew ever louder until they joined up to make a circle; like a magnetic track of pain which attracted all motives and all thoughts and spun harder, harder!

I *wanted* the pain to be real! I wanted the stab to be some physical misfortune! that would give dignity to all this howling. For what explanation could I give anyone were I to stop now as I needed to; were I to beg now as I wanted to; were I to collapse now as might have been better for me? What could I say? I could scarcely speak. Only now can I approach a description of what then I was: only now can I hope to give you some notion of it. At the time I was suffering and unable to describe it, consumed by the effort needed to tolerate it. You can only surrender if the rules allow it: you can only lean on the world if you know that the world recognizes you to be lame. I was whole. I had a brown carrier-bag. I was walking up the High Street past the

Blue Star Garage as might any man of thirty, university-educated and soberly dressed down to the sandals. Why do I insist so on dress? Perhaps because the clothes held me in place. Inside them I was at least at some point.

I did want the pain to be real. Not yet was I wanting to die. But these tremors and disturbances had been around me, had played with me for months now; ever since the move. And since my best friend and his wife had left London to teach abroad. I had once spent a good deal of time with them. They welcomed me to their flat in the suburb. I helped them to accommodate to the loneliness of an indigent and early marriage I suppose: they were both friends and family to me. It was their departure which had finally determined my own. Since then, I'd been preyed on by these upsets, these nightmares from the past leaking through to the present like gas, ready to be ignited and blow off that cover of repression and new habit.

Again and again these wounds which left no mark attacked my body. I bought the cake: a pineapple cake. The distance between myself and the girl who took the money was oceanic. Perhaps with their minute brains and the pressure and uniformity of the water fish or reptiles are as distant from each other when they pass and cannot measure presence in its fullness.

Perfectly normally I went to the café I always went to on Saturday mornings—the one with the seats outside—and ordered my usual black coffee. I write 'my usual'—usual to me alone. The waitresses changed weekly (always long-legged, always untroubled) and though there were a few real 'regulars', they obviously came more than merely once a week. Perhaps they were writers or actors 'resting'. Why, why do I speculate so when I am trying to tell you of the distance between myself and that steaming cup, of the thankfulness I felt when I sipped and it slightly scalded my tongue?

I sipped again and began one of the simple 'games'

or trials that I was to play all day: I counted to twenty-five in quarters, halves, threequarters and whole numbers. Reckoning it would take me about a minute to get there and that would be one minute longer.

There was nowhere calling me in London. No one onto whom I could dump this body with its internal lacerations. I *could* have gone back home. That word. To my mother. I could have caught one of the fast trains from Euston and been in Cumberland in five hours. I wanted to avoid that. Even when I thought I was dying? And wanting to die?

But all the day it remained a possibility and on one screen of my mind the view from the train was projected: the layers of railway lines at Crewe, the chimney-pots and archetypal industrial streets of Wigan, and then the slow mounting of Shap Fell, whale-backed hills bare and tranquil as a mind could be among them, and the race, the tumble, the charge down into Cumberland.

The youth—the 'tough' I called him in my first notes—he'd not followed me. I had turned before going into the cake shop and seen him still on the corner: looking in my direction, yes, but the distance neutralized the effect of that stare. He'd frightened me, though: yet, like the nerve in my eye, there was some relief in such an obvious cause of disturbance.

Ought I to try to tell you of the long build-up to this day? Of the previous times my self had slid off me? I could not do that with sufficient interest because though reasons stated in such a fashion might be informative they would not convince you as I hope this fiction will. I must concentrate it in that one day. No tuning up, no overture. No energy for that. And did it happen on one day? Not all—no: but enough, God yes; enough happened on that day: sometimes great things do happen on a day. We die on a day and are born on another. Whoever wanted that day? And after that bloody ejection, to be slapped into life and welcomed only when we scream. Is it any wonder: after that, is anything a wonder? The whole point about my reasons is that they are common reasons. I will try to keep to that while I concentrate more and more on myself as I must to develop the day now: because not only were there internal wars, the world outside was assembling forces.

I wish I *could* remember that book. I read it, and counted in fractions and saw Shap Fell; the nerve flickered and 'the tough' was still there—I would have to pass him again. Parts of books I'd read, words I'd heard spoken—words I'd intended to speak, a lecture on 'The Artist as Pulse and Parasite'—I jotted down the title: it was physically difficult to write. I noticed that, helplessly; as if the biro were a tool which I had not yet mastered.

Words are all I can produce. In this place they guide me to myself. My father used to finish a day's work (so he told me; and I believed him), and then bike eight or nine miles to dance reels and schottisches (before that ceremony which bound him to house and home): he went through life with his skin near his spirits. I do not use my body to make a passage: I talk my way through. Sometimes it is as he described it when he said, 'You got so that you could not stop: you went on working and rushing out and playing football and dancing: you were frightened to stop.' His excesses were physical: mine are verbal: neither road seems to have led to wisdom. Why was he *frightened* to stop?

The thighs went by and I sipped my cooling coffee. The young men in carnival dress and the older men in a sort of urban beachwear. How can lust be appeased when it is so diversely, so insistently, aroused? *I* sat there, a credit to the system: in dress and manner, in attitude and thoughts; look at my bank account; slice open my skull—I had done everything I 'ought': I had done everything that society had directed. And I was without grace.

* * * *

A General Confession.

'Almighty and most merciful Father; we have erred and strayed from Thy ways like lost sheep. We have followed too much the devices and desires of our own hearts. We have offended against Thy holy laws. We have left undone those things which we ought to have done: and we have done those things which we ought not to have done: and there is no health in us. But Thou, O Lord, have mercy upon us, miserable offenders. Spare Thou them, O God, which confess their faults. Restore Thou them that are penitent: according to Thy promises declared unto mankind in Christ Jesu our Lord. And grant, O most merciful Father, for his sake; that we may hereafter live a godly, righteous and sober life, to the glory of Thy holy name. Amen.'

The shuffle of knees on hassocks and the voices above a whisper but quieter than in conversation. It makes sense now. Christianity contains metaphors for all of my life: and Christ's existence is both a symbol and an example; a parable.

If only I believed; but am without grace.

* * * *

'Come on, Johnson, come on. *How* much do you do? Four hours a night? Five, six? Do you stay up all night . . . ? Guys who have to swot *that* hard are generally thick. Not you. Generally speaking. How much, Ted?'

It was a mistake for me to come out of the library for a mid-morning cup of coffee. It was the smart thing to do if you were seventeen or eighteen and working for your 'A' level exams. You came to the town's library on Saturday mornings and with much giggling and affectations of boredom and indifference anxiously smuggled your way through an hour's work and THEN—Rod, always Rod—Rod would stretch and yawn and crack his fingers and wink at the High School girls (our segregated counterparts) who'd pretend to resent his frivolity (how hard they seemed to work—eyes down; navy blue cardigans clinging to the bended backs). Then, most gracefully, Rod the Captain of Rugby and Cricket and idly clever, would lunge himself forward from the tippling chair and lounge out of the library looking compassionately at that row of sad old men in raincoats who sat before the big wooden panels which held the daily newspapers. The others followed.

Only a few remained. Some girls and Ted. Myself. I see myself as another in that large room—like a railway waiting room: and my books so neatly laid out. Losing ground. Already I was hating them: no not them, not the books: myself as their creature, myself as an identity only through the books.

'Four Eyes.'

'Swot.'

'Speccy.' Speccy, Speccy, Speccy.

'Butter Fingers.' Can't hold a catch.

I enjoyed sport but was nervous and allowed myself to be laughed out of it: they were kinder to me on the sports field than anywhere else: they would explain how I ought to play (I *knew* how to play): they would lob me cissy passes and tackle me gently. I was not talented enough to survive such indulgences. With tender sympathy, they saw me off.

Sometimes I joined them for coffee.

I resented paying ninepence for a cup of sludge in a basement and sixpence for the two biscuits that somehow HAD to go with it. One and three would have bought me . . . nothing much; but I carried echoes of parental consternation about the Value of Money and the Days when a shilling could, virtually, take you around the country.

I knew they would pick on me and they always did. I was easy to pick on. I was definitely what I was—a Swot. I accentuated the gawpiness which alone made it tolerable to them. Without their having the wit to recognize it, I played the clown for them. They wanted to see scholarship as a fool and mock it and for that reason they liked me to join them in the basement.

They would always ask the same questions. I used to remember a novel where the men used to ask this young man how often he 'got it'. Rod's questions were like that and the contrast and yet the similarity crosses my mind now and perhaps did then: something had to sustain it because though I played a fool, I was not a fool: yet they took me for a fool.

'How much a night?'

'Oh,' I would say, holding back the gift until the beneficiaries were suitably primed to receive it, 'no *regular* amount.' Which was a lie.

'Old Ted,' said Rod, who led the hunt as he led everything: as he was to lead the examination results because he slaved in secret more than any of us as he has since 'divulged': most delightedly. 'Old Ted,' and he would hunch over the narrow table in that posh basement where my mother would fear to tread, it being for 'students' and those middle-class ladies of the town who used the morning's shopping as an excuse for this chatty coffee, 'Old Ted does so much reading that his eyes see everything in print, don't they Ted? When he sees a female, he doesn't see 36-22-36—not Ted: he sees the word FEMALE—he does! It's like that for everything, isn't it Ted? Come on, you sly old bugger—how much a night?'

There was real anxiety in his question. He told me later

51

that he used me as his yardstick. I misinterpreted the anxiety as simple cruelty: which it was only in part. 'Say four.' I hesitated: let them have it. 'Five, more like.'

And oh the fun they had with that!

'Tell us something new, Ted,' Rod would ask when they'd dried their eyes. And like the pup's tail, I would wag. 'Well, I was reading about the Aztecs the other night.'

'They're not on the syllabus!'

'Who does he play for?'

'Christ!'

'AS—who?'

'Shut up!' Rod *wanted* to know. He treated me as a tap to be turned on; for the little sips I gave him were carefully stored in one of his humps and used to good effect, later. 'What about the Aztecs, Ted?'

'Well for one thing they believed that this present age had been preceded by other distinct epochs.'

'Who doesn't?'

'Who does Epoch play for?'

'SHUT UP YOU BONE-Heads! Listen to the guy. Go on Ted.'

'Well—the thing is, all of these other epochs had ended catastrophically. This was the concept of 'Suns' —the sun was central to it all—or worlds, each one following the other. Now the interesting thing is that they, too, thought that *they* would be destroyed. Like our Millenialists.'

'Who does *he* play for?' A most subdued mutter by now; disappearing at a glance.

'Each Epoch has lasted a complete period consisting of a fixed number of cycles of fifty-two years—the Aztec 'centuries'—and for this reason the end of the world was feared at the conclusion of these calendrical periods. During the last night of a cycle, while waiting for the arrival of the light of the new day, the priests followed the course of the stars. When the Pleiades passed the zenith, it was believed that the fortune of the current generation had been decided on favourably, and that the Gods had granted the earth fifty-two more years of life. Divine favour was bought with the hearts and blood of men that found the new sun through the rite of human sacrifice. Only the nobles could be sacrificed. The rich.'

They would drift off, all but Rod; and I would waste a precious hour in telling more to Rod. He was the only one I could tell it to. I found it difficult to bring it into general essays and discussions as he did, to drop it in, casually, with never a blush. I thought of him as a thief then, but when he pressed me I would tell him more.

Rod got into Oxford; I failed that. At Bristol I lost much of the pleasure I'd had in my own subject: I was more interested to read up other subjects in my own way. Both Rod and I ended up with Second Class Honours Degrees: his more impressive than mine, of course, being from Oxford.

He had one thing he used to say, often said it, which irritated me without fail. He must have known that. 'Good old Ted,' he would say. 'Good old Ted; ask him what Tutenkhamen did to Nefertiti!'

Rod lives in Hampstead—in style. He used to come to that coffee place sometimes. I'm ashamed to tell you that's why I went to it so regularly. Hoping to see him: to be included in his success.

Tutenkhamen. Nefertiti.

*   *   *   *

Geoffrey spoke mischievously—exaggerating and aping what he thought he represented to people like me. He liked me but was wary; especially in public. And yet the public nature of this meeting, the street, the people, urged him on. He liked his part and played at playing it.

Besides, he liked to tease us others by overdoing it. We were tested that way.

'What's wrong with your face?'

Something 'nudged my elbow'. Even in the state I was I could recognize the nervous affectation of the gesture: or perhaps this is hindsight. What I want you to know is that the tone of the voice, the use of the word 'face' instead of 'eye', the ridge of embarrassment which Geoffrey seemed to raise before himself, peeping over it now timidly, now cheekily—all this helped. Geoffrey was an actor—out of work at the moment—and he lived downstairs from me with Harold, an accountant. So I was acquainted with him. And some coincidence between the tepidity of my relationship to him and the stratagems of his behaviour made him the very person I could talk to. For the subversion which he thought necessary for his life in some way found a likeness in the screens which shifted in my head, now hiding me, now exposing me, now brilliantly lit, now black, now streaked with hopelessness, now blank. My attention was all but fully concentrated on what I was: as was his. So we communicated through screens of false selves.

'Your face, Teddy': my complaint gave him the excuse for intimacy it seemed.

'Do you mind if I sit down? Ta. What's wrong with it?'

I explained about the nerve.

'Oh, you poor thing. You should bathe it. Use that Milton and a hot flannel. Or witch-hazel; that's very underrated I think. Let's have a look: take your hand away, I won't scratch it out. I'm good at this sort of thing.'

And his scrubbed white fingers with fingernails so immaculate they looked false *were* tender on the swollen spot. 'Shouldn't be surprised if its full of pus. The badness coming out in you! *Poor* old thing. Why don't you go to a doctor?'

I shook my head.

'I don't blame you. They know nothing nowadays: nothing. *Really*. Harold went for his back—I smile but I kid you not—you know, one of those cricks at the bottom of the spine—really *pain*ful. And she said it was with too much sitting down! Harold! He does those Canadian Air Force exercises every morning and we walk all around the Heath twice every weekend. He'd *pulled* something. She wouldn't even have known what came and what went down there, stupid old cow. They're just labourers, you know, these G.P.s nowadays. I mean, they can spot a broken leg at about five yards but be a bit more subtle and it's Harley Street and ten guineas or lame for life. Coffee? Coffee please, miss. Yes. White? Two white. You'd think they'd serve black *or* white, you know, like in France where they bring independent pots and you can choose on the spot without having to send a postcard like here. Don't you think English people are lazy? Oh, it's all right, freedom and that sort of thing, but they're LAZY, aren't they? You should get yourself a pair of sunglasses. Woolworths have some very nice copies of expensive ones very cheap.'

He chattered away: perhaps he knew that this was what I needed. I dipped into his monologue and out of it, like a radio station you keep switching past as you turn the dial. He reminded me of my father. And, as with my father, I was somehow unsexed.

My father would sit as Geoffrey was sitting—fixed on the small thing to hand, the cup, the piece of wood he was whittling, the length of string, and talk to me ceaselessly, humbly and pliantly as if his whole purpose were to bring me news as armies are brought supplies. Dominating by service.

My departure for university had finished us. He greeted my return as that of a welcome stranger come

55

to lodge with him and full of inaccessible stores of power and learning; so formidable that the only way to cope was to construct a defence and the only defences were not to speak at all (his preferred method), or not to allow me to speak. Here, he was like Geoffrey whose monologue had a different cause—he wanted an audience whereas my father wanted no play—but the pain and the effect were the same. And I was unsexed because I could not find my rôle. My father did not want me to be his son: the rivalry of a son distressed him. I was no friend, no brother; and when I made any gestures or assumptions which called into the open our blood relationship, he would flinch so that I would feel protective, womanly. In some way he saw this both as the surest ground for himself and as the territory which made me most squirm: he emphasized his own softness and demanded more womanly concern by himself becoming less and less manly.

There have been periods—of abstinence—when I've thought of the definitions of sex in terms half-fearful, half-playful. No man I know is not attracted to other men: the attraction is often warm, sometimes intense. That it is generally directed in a platonic direction is supposed to be to do with something in ourselves as well as with others : biology as much as society. But what of the times when your emotions are disrupted? Is that a time of truth or of deceit?

As then, that day, while Geoffrey chatted on and I saw my father, the neb of his cap pulled down towards his large nose, his thick fingers shaving the wood expertly and gently and me wanting to put my arms around him: or have him do that to me: or have something else but these two men we were, obstructing the flow that should and could have been between us. So, in reminding me, Geoffrey called out the same uncertainties—if uncertainty needed hailing on that day—why do we

56

divide between Man and Woman in matters of the affections? Why cannot a man be comforting without being womanly? It is at the edge, at the brink that you consider divisions as arbitary which are fundamental to nature itself. When your own nature has failed.

'You *are*, though. You're *very* well built. I've seen you coming out of that bathroom of yours; good deltoids and strong lateral muscles : biceps a bit thin but strong forearms. I used to do body-building, did you know that? That was where I met Harold. He came to take it up but he never did. Mind you, you get out of shape so quickly.'

He stretched—to show his perfect shape in the yellow T-shirt and bright blue jeans divided by a compact stomach girded with a rope belt, and his image changed to that of my father sitting opposite me. As in a hallucination. My father was sitting there. I prayed that Geoffrey would talk on and give me time to deal with this. My legs went stiff with tension and I felt my chest tighten, rigidly.

'You have, though,' said my father, 'you've done very well. I've seen you working in that bedroom of yours, a good lad you are, working away there, and I say to all of them that asks—and there's plenty remember you—I say, "He's worked for what he's got": "I don't grudge him it,' I say, "nobody's helped him but hissel." I say, "I couldn't help him—that's a fact; that's something doesn't need proving. What a lad for getting stuck in, he is," I say. I say, "He'll can do whatever he'll set his mind to with a mind like that." I tell them all.'

I dare not close my eyes for then the swayboats of mind would sweep me into emptiness as just before sickness in drink.

Then Geoffrey left. Perhaps he saw my state and saw how best to help. He patted my arms, told me to cheer up, invited me to drop in and see them 'any time'; and

57

left the one-and-sixpence for his coffee neatly stacked under the saucer.

* * * *

The flood down the narrow valley; the pent-up force of water thrusting down the gorge. The dam has burst, the rain keeps falling, and with it the flood brings houses and trees and rocks and animals, bushes and shacks and fences and birds, debris and rubbish and the occasional piece preserved, afloat and unharmed: and sometimes a corpse.

* * * *

Let us say that my father's retreat forced me to advance. Let us be military here in this place my home, where we have a routine. We have breakfast at 7.30: we have lunch at 12.00: we have tea at 3.30: we have dinner at 6.30: we are offered cocoa and biscuits at 9.30. And we enjoy it!

The only way to train animals is to work them at their feeding times.

* * * *

How can my father be responsible for that period in my life when I kept 'testing' myself? It *might*, on some principle of equilibrium, have been my attempt to reassert masculinity. But timid young pimps and frightened old whores go in dockside bars, too: and come out unchanged and unchallenged, as I did.

Here in London I've been in the tough districts: along the docks—embarrassed, somehow, at so exploiting their public reputation for my own private reassurance. I saw other men fight; and was both excited, afraid and sickened. Mostly sickened, I believe. There was no skill beyond that shrewdness given by desperation; no elegance—only gasping and yelping and viciousness: the

58

thud of a boot in the side. I went into the West Indian area in Notting Hill where some pubs are like shebeens and it's as if the negative has been reversed: for suddenly *you* are the odd one and black is right. They talked about bad housing and I went back with an old man, grey-haired and unbitter, and saw a four-storey house such as the one I inhabit: this one was lived in by twenty-nine people sharing three kitchens and two lavatories (one bust). I wandered around Piccadilly after midnight and up into Soho and was one of the scores of tourists looking for frisson; for a reason to jump off the pavement with a tickle of nervous delight. I went to Hammersmith Palais and there indeed was most scared when a gang from Fulham took on some boys from Cricklewood and then the bouncers came in ('Can't hit them 'till they start, see: gotta wait, see: aggravating sometimes'), and these ex-prizefighters scythed their way down the gleaming dance floor like hoplites levelling an unworthy enemy. It was in the West London press the next day but no mention in the Nationals.

Does this catalogue seem to slide over the truth? Like those who come out of strip shows and say they were 'bored', that is only part of it: for though they might have been bored by the end, they say nothing of the drill of pleasurable expectation which had sunk into them to get them there, nor the suspense of the titillation, the gregarious unease, the stingless shadiness of it all, the vicarious, stealing, lustful, criminality of desire in illicit surroundings. Similar is my catalogue of those times I sought to test myself.

But throughout this story I am met by such problems which other writers can 'solve'. On one level, writing is a form of engineering even though the struts should not show: some do, deliberately, from another philosophy. My problem is to transfer to you a degree of intensity. A page or so ago I wrote of the routine in this place. That is both a relief and an imprisonment: always I am glad to hear the food-bell and always there is the pitch of fear as at the sound of the rattling of chains. It is a house of ease, this routine, laid out like a palace of comfort: and yet it is also the fortress which captures myself.

Again, the whole of this record, this book, this story is being written in coherent sentences yet the time was one, largely, of incoherence. I can see no solution to that: breaking up the matter of the communication, as William Burroughs does, makes for a different strain than the one intended; the strain of following the intention of the writer and not the writing, the teller, not the tale. While working from example, the best record of incoherence I know comes in Tolstoy where Anna Karenina breaks down. Lucid. Coherent. More important, though more difficult, is the fact that the very sentence structure, vocabulary and frame of implication I employ calls on a tradition and a culture which I think my own small revulsion was to some extent both caused by and directed against. That is what one of my lectures was about; or, rather, that is what I have since discovered it to be about—I have it here and leaf through it sometimes. That way madness. My revolt was against the lid of the past which had been placed on me, which I had pulled down over my eyes and clung to and sheltered under and used as a form for growth but which was not what I wanted, did not match what I was. Like a skin graft which does not take, it began by sweating and then the pain. It would not take: nor did I want it to. I preferred myself with scars. They had to be discovered.

*   *   *   *

So with those adventures by night. Perhaps if I'd gone by day it would have been more satisfactory. When I first went into the East End, I remembered

60

Charles Dickens meeting two or three policemen to tour the destitute districts: that seemed to be voyeuristic, though justified by his novels, where he used it and humanized it. On the contrary, I thought, my quest was real. It was to see how much I dared. To discover the extent of my territory by uncovering its boundaries.

Perhaps I wanted to be hurt and then I would have had an unimpeachable excuse for withdrawal from the real world.

Looking back now, I guess that a certain cunning (though then unconscious) naïvety saved me the slightest trouble. I dressed as I always did—like a quiet civil servant in his time off. I drank halves of bitter and took a book to occupy myself with in moments of boredom. I always carried a raincoat, a rather battered one I'd had since university days, and of course there was my first line of defence—my spectacles.

I might as well have been a table or a chair in most places.

I took great care not to 'eye' any of the women, let me tell you that. None.

So I didn't dare very much. But at least I discovered a further remoteness in myself: I could not find a limit perhaps because there was no territory to be conserved.

Not once, not one anecdote from all those excursions? No. Even the preparatory thrills of fear, when I would get off the bus or out of the tube and walk through empty streets shining black from the rain and see clumps of youths growing out of a fish-and-chip shop or listen to the internal combustion of a pub or hear deformed footsteps behind me or go into the white electric mouth of a south London Saturday-night dance hall or not find a seat in a bar and stand with my half bitter being bumped by other customers who were ready to believe that *I* was bumping *them*—even those times, O Lord, lost their zest.

Other tests seemed more fearful then: the trial of

61

how long I could go on three hours sleep a night; the cutting down of food (after reading Simone Weil); the intensive reading programmes (all forgot: they should supply a certificate guaranteeing the properties of memory to those willing to embark on a learning process; a brain check). If you have lived alone or found yourself lonely, or discovered yourself in a new world of mind or a new spot physically, then you know the ways adopted to find your place and, once found, to work outwards again, draw the map, finger the mountain and trace out the villages with fingers gradually losing their blindness until you are again located.

But then, in that coffee place, and now, later still, writing this, I longed and long for that physical carelessness or confidence, that inviolability or invulnerability I once had. Auden somewhere describes himself in the company of criminals—unharmed—because, he says, he was pure in heart and 'Blessed are the pure in heart.' I was never pure and am willing to accept my fears now of my mother's coming and my fears then of that young tough's staring, as the brain's infection from the poisons of impurity. Fear is in the fall.

*　　*　　*　　*

I'm very tired tonight. I've been writing on and off for over a fortnight now and though I've nothing else to do here it's still very tiring. The more I say the more there *is* to say. Yet I will not let it spread much further than my original intention: it will be short.

I want to get back to myself in that coffee house waiting for Rod, hoping and I think willing Rod to turn up.

'Ted looks ill,' I could hear him say: I hoped to hear him say. 'Dear old Ted looks really rather serious. Oughtn't we to . . . Ted? Ted?'

Echoes in the empty wells of mind: the shafts of

thought: the doors of perception. Entrances all: no exits. Holes into tunnels: no light at the end.

I want to sleep now: but there is one final thing I must get down today. My right eye has started to flicker: it has started to 'go' like the left eye of the man in the story. Which is both compliance and contradiction. Or coincidence.

I am very tired.

The nurse gave me some cream to put on it and she told me I was 'wasting' too much time at that table; 'whatever you're doing there.' I lied to her and said I was making notes for a talk: had I said I was writing a story, she'd have wanted me to read it to her. She's very jolly: very cheerful; she would have given me no rest if I'd told her I was writing a story.

Despite the salve, my eye hurts and I'm afraid I'll have to ask for a sleeping pill. I'd given them up.

*   *   *   *

1 a.m.

When I close my eyes and listen, I think I can remember most of what he said. It may be a fantasy or a dream but I've had to get up and jot it down. It must fit in with the story or it wouldn't have been hammering in my head for these last two hours. You become immune to the effects of sleeping pills.

It is a man at the café. With a loud voice, a young man with an orange satin shirt and white jeans, rope sandals and exposed toe-nails, a 'strapping' young man with a silk scarf and fair hair carefully brushed, I guessed, with ivory-backed brushes from New Bond Street; one of the young men from that lush reach of stockbroker-Hampstead, I would have said; well-schooled though a little lacking in native wit; well groomed though, again, lacking in natural attraction: with a very loud voice: talking to an extremely beautiful girl who looked eighteen and had blonde hair which tumbled all over her bra-less breasts. Shouting at her.

'The *great* thing about the I.C.I.,' he said—and as I remember he elaborated on the initials—'Imperial Chemical Industries,' and paused, 'the *great* thing about the I.C.I. is that they really look after their chaps. I mean, you know: reasonable rents. They let 'em know how the firm's doing; they give 'em *pride* in the place, you see? Result? Second to none. Lead the world. Ask any of these chaps who *know*. They'll tell you—second to one. And the *rugger* pitches!

'We played their firsts on the tour—they wanted us to play their seconds but we said "No, old chaps: firsts or not at all." Well we got there. They have two full county caps and three trialists in their firsts, you know. They play all these cracking Northern teams. And I tell *you*, girl; they're tough up there in the North. Rugger's rugger in that part of the world.'

And the girl listening Intent. Deeper breaths as she summoned all to concentrate on this bore who had it in his pocket to enable her to live richly ever after. Was that it? Sports cars and dining out—that is the way; daddies and flower shows, whatever they say; bank account, cash no bar; go to Harrods too; all kinds of wise advice—leads her to you or perhaps she was being polite. Those heavier breaths parted the blonde hair and I saw the nipples; a deep and greedy brown.

'They had thirty rugger pitches on one—you might say—field: more like a park. Thirty! Possibly there were more. And that *club*house! I tell you—I'll wager it's no better at Twickenham. No. In fact, I'd wager dear old Twickers could learn a thing or two from the I.C.I. They have a fully qualified staff of gardeners—God knows how many—more than the Queen or some damned thing—anyway all these chaps keep the pitches like bowling greens. They have all the latest stuff, you see. I.C.I. do fertilizers and, you know, insecticide stuff—all that stuff that makes farming such a doddle nowadays. The Danes use it a lot, I'm told. And the showers! I've *never* been in showers like that! You should've seen ours at school! Ha! Good Lord, I couldn't begin to describe them!

'These chaps have showers like ... like ... you know —*magnificent*. So I said to some of the chaps after the game—casually you know, doesn't do to be obvious at this sort of thing—I said, "What chance a solicitor chappie like myself getting employ with the old I.C.I.? Purely as a matter of interest."

'And lo and behold, their stand-off had known a chap I'd known at school and both of them were in the place as solicitors beavering away like beavers. The thing is, you see ...' his voice dropped and he glanced across at me suspiciously: the girl leaned forward in response to him and I saw strands of the blonde hair shimmer in the sun: such a perfect skin, she had, and that sweep of jaw which makes your fingers ache to touch it and follow the line of it.... 'The thing is, you see, these chappies go into I.C.I., get all their training and experience in the industrial gubbins at I.C.I.'s expense —then they push off into private practice and make an absolute bomb.... I'm thinking that one out for myself.'

He swung upright and she snapped to attention just as neatly as he. A glance got her moving and he ushered her small backside before him. She passed me and I stared. He passed me and said: 'Did you get it all down?'

* * * *

'What's the matter with your eye?'

I explained.

'Well, they tell me you've been writing. Nurse White says you're writing a book.'

I denied it.

'We needn't talk if you don't want to. You know that. Not feeling like talking today . . . ?'

'No. No thanks.' We both paused: but I meant it.

'Fine. See Nurse White about that eye, though. Your mother will be after me if we appear to be neglecting you. Good afternoon.'

My mother and the doctor had a pleasant relationship: bantering, mutually respectful. I like him, too.

*　　*　　*　　*

'What's the matter with your eye?'

I explained.

'You've been slogging away too hard, I know. A monograph on Ming porcelain this time?'

I denied it.

'Have another coffee?'

Rod sat down beside me and I could have cried with relief. But of course the 'rule' was not only to conceal that at all costs but even to contradict it by affecting mild surprise and indifference.

'Rod,' I wanted to say, 'just for today let's forget the game we play which anyway is becoming tedious to you and rather desperate for me. You're becoming well-known, with your television show and your "touch" in other things: you don't need me. You seem to keep me on as a reminder: looking at me you can see how far you've gone. And you still play the game of my being the sedulous scholar as stuffed with odd bits as a Christmas chicken—remember when you said that? Why did you choose "chicken"?

'I need help. If I ask you for it you will try to give it but it will be the end. I will have embarrassed you and threatened your liberty, my tyranny. I want you to feel it as I sit here. We know each other well enough, don't we? You can tell: can't you see on my face that inside the skin, the cells multiply and die? That I am now wrecked on some rocks of myself and am shaking in the gale? You once saw me with Lizzie. I introduced her to you and you were charming as usual and she was very thrilled. Really. Already then you could impress people in a few minutes. I bet she boasts of it now—to her girl friends. I even told you—one recent drunken night—how uneasily do I get drunk; how gracelessly! I told you I had loved this one girl and you guessed who it was, though you'd only met her once, and I told you how *much* I loved her still!

'If we talk about her now perhaps the baby will not come back into my throat.

'Rod, I don't want to be "swot" or "old Ted" any more: I am not like that. *You* begin: *you* begin by treating me as you find me. Find me. Find me.'

'Sugar?'

'Yes.' Scarcely audible: each word was pushed up my gorge, as painful as a scrap of food being slowly hawked up. 'Two, isn't it? You brain drains need all the energy you can get. Though I must say it never shows on you. You've become quite a fit-looking guy over the last year or so, Ted. What's the secret?'

I shook my head. Rod leaned back, patted a scarcely visible stomach and politely offered me a cigarette though he knew I didn't smoke.

'I'm going to hell,' he said. Then, in the Cumbrian dialect he sometimes affected and which made me writhe—what *right* had he to play around with it? He'd never spoken it as a child as I had. His father was a grinning golfing grey-haired doctor, thank you very much. Christ! How I hated his using that dialect. It was as if he were caricaturing my father. 'Thou knows, Ted lad, we'll hev te git summat dun aboot this belly o' mine afoor it's ower big te put intil a pair o' pants.'

I laughed: or imitated a laugh. He was a good mimic. Others at other tables were ruffled by it too: even such a tiny performance had found an audience: he was (in a small, 'English' way) a recognized figure in Hampstead. People expected things from him.

He gulped his coffee. He was always in a rush. 'What's that you're reading?' He took the book from me and skimmed through a few pages.

What was the title?

'Any good?'

'I haven't started it.'

I remember saying that. If I'd admitted having read it, I'd have had to give him a précis and then been cross-examined on it. He still used me as an encyclopaedia. 'You were reading Wordsworth when I last saw you. I haven't read him since we were at school. Remember Mr Blacker reciting it in his best tight-lipped Yorkshire? He was a good teacher: never forced anything. What happened to Wordsworth?'

I had to find a quick way out: he would have me explaining the relevance of Wordsworth to this, that and everything if I didn't side-step quickly.

'He died, just like everybody else.' Lame. But it worked.

'Keeping it to yourself till you publish your collected thoughts eh? The little scarlet book of Chairman Ted. Is that John Neville?'

'Who?'

'John Neville. Used to be a star at the Old Vic—ran the Nottingham Playhouse. . . .'

I *knew* who John Neville was! My reaction had nothing to do with the information.

'Why?'

'I want to talk to him about this idea I have. . . .' He jumped up. '. . . For a programme,' he added, apologetically: but either some hint of my need finally got through to him or because he wanted to compensate me for loping off to 'better pastures', or as a result of genuine, general largesse which could so easily sound so patronizing, he stopped a moment longer and said, 'I've a party tonight. Come along. About ten. Bring a bird or don't. Doesn't matter. There'll be plenty of "lawse".' He used the Cumbrian word, meaning loose, spare, available. 'Lots o' lawse!' he repeated smiling and left me—dodging through the traffic, at one with the pageant moving up and down the High Street, part—solidly and indubitably part of that display, that crowd, that London scene: running down his quarry.

And I alone to cross that gulf of traffic and return to the empty flat. No comedy. No self-pity, either. It is strange: I have been prone to it but there was very little on that day. Fear drove it out.

I waited and sipped at the coffee. And still the world crawled into my head.

3

'You're looking better.'

She always said that.

'Yes. You're looking much better. You still don't put any weight on, though. Nurse White says you only eat half what they give you.'

To my mother a hospital is a hospital and a patient is ill: I was not a voluntary inmate at an 'open' clinic but a convalescent in a Home. She was Lowland Scots and the burr still remained though she'd moved to Cumberland when she was fourteen.

'You ought to eat it all. They cook it well. I've seen the kitchens. They do it very carefully.' And those three last syllables were drawn from her throat as precisely as she drew the dove-grey gloves off her fingers.

'Well! Let's have some fresh air.'

She went to the window and opened it. Outside was a bright midwinter day. All the grounds bare and the trees empty, the lawns dull and the flower beds earth only. Above, a glittering copper disc of sun with little power to warm this day.

'We could go out for a walk.'

We went out for a walk.

I held her arm and yet it could appear that she was supporting me. She was wearing her smart grey coat which had once fitted perfectly, I knew, but now hung on the wasting body. A black hat, black scarf, black shoes—'Black looks smart with anything,' she'd say: but the gloves were dove-grey for fear, I thought; for fear of being too funeral when coming to see me. She would sacrifice elegance for my comfort—any time. Any sacrifice; any time.

'But mother, I'm a man not a god, and don't need a sacrifice. It does not strengthen me, your blood. It does not replenish my veins and feed me as you think or hope it does. I see the act and am unhappy and the weight of my sadness is like a leaden collar. When you come I let you slip on the leash because I love you despite your love for me. I know that you sometimes realize how long ago your sacrifice became myself.'

And a black bag: I'd bought her that.

'This bag you bought me; it's worn so well. I wrap it up every time after I use it, but even so.'

It was real leather and she showed it to me as if it were new again and asked me to rub it between finger and thumb.

We came to the lake where the ducks huddled close to the verge. I didn't know the name of the species, or is it breed or type, of duck? Some had green heads, some brown, mostly grey and black—but some with beautiful patterns: and I stood and observed them as ignorantly as a child while my mother took out a small package of greaseproof paper and uncovered some bread which she fed them bit by bit.

'They're lovely, aren't they?' She smiled: all lovely things made her smile. I had to turn away; my own weakness could bring me near to tears when I looked at her and realized how few times I'd see her again. She would excuse the tears.

The sound of the ducks was loud in the grounds. Few of the patients had come out on this cold afternoon. I wore no coat.

(I must remember to emphasize the *heat* of that Saturday I write of: the terrible heat which began to hit me in my own room and already in that café was causing me to run with sweat down the armpits; my brow was damp.)

71

I was cold but I enjoyed being cold: the heat of my room would then seem cosy and not stuffy.

'The doctor told me about your eye. That's why I didn't ask when I came in. He said it would make you self-conscious of it, so I kept it back. Does it hurt?'

'No.'

'It *looks* painful. Won't the cold make it worse?'

'Fresh air'll do it good.'

'Yes.'

We walked towards the azalea grove. It must be like a tropical island there in the summer. She stepped out briskly. Perhaps I had just imagined she was dying, or perhaps it was an unconscious wish, the only way my chaos could see an end. But the doctor *had* confirmed it. I pictured the scene in my mind again, as we walked to the bare azalea grove; to be certain.

He had been in his white housecoat standing against a white wall.

'What reason can you have for *not* telling me?'

'She spoke to me in confidence.'

'You've answered my question by your evasion. She *is* dying, isn't she?'

'Is it very painful for you not to know?'

'I won't be able to bear it. I'll pester you or I'll blurt it out to her. I'm no good at enduring things.'

'I gave her my word.'

'So she is: you don't shake your head. She *is*. No more said.'

She had once been plump and when I was about fourteen she'd got her promotion to become 'school secretary'. She'd been happy then and taught me Scottish dancing in the kitchen when Jimmy Shand played on the radio. I would soon forget my embarrassment and we'd whirl about until the music stopped or my father came in. He'd always looked old enough to be *her* father.

Her step even now was lively: her mother, whom I'd

72

sometimes remember vividly, wore long skirts and would perhaps have been praised for a 'lively ankle'. My mother's brisk step helped me imagine how sweet that sight could have been.

In the azalea grove we met the doctor and she blushed as if she'd been caught out. Just the mildest of blushes: scarcely enlivening that white, tightening skin: but I noticed it who noticed everything about her.

'I didn't think you were a man for exercise, doctor,' she said, in a broader accent than usual—memory, perhaps, being used to drive out desire—'I'd thought of you more as a man at a desk.'

While I'd been in the place I'd let my hair grow: it was not shoulder-length, nowhere near, but it was long and thick; rather surprisingly, the length had discovered waves which I'd never thought I had. And somehow by combining trousers from one suit with a battered jacket and an Indian shirt I'd been given by a girl friend long ago and put away until now, in some way, I felt—I who am looking for a style—I felt very easy and even elegant: though borrowed from contemporary casualness it was helping me to become what I might be. All this is to cover the tone in which doctor and mother exchanged gentle and proud remarks about my appearance. My mother now pleased now chiding; the doctor managing to talk to her without patronizing her; but nor did he chill her remarks and so isolate them as the rather foolish old saws they were.

She became 'serious'.

'How many of your patients left this week, doctor?'

'Let's see . . . four.'

'Permanent?'

'Two of them.'

'There'll be two more in the queue to take their place no doubt?'

'Yes. There are always more.'

'Your work'll not be done until there's no queue at

all, doctor. And then you'll have no work. Would you welcome that?'

How firmly she stood! Still finding room for movement despite the locks and chains of her past and the certainty so near. How interested she was in the hospital: it might have been the school.

She'd retired from the school, she said. I knew that her illness made it impossible for her to carry on. And when she came, increasingly I recognized the effort in the over-bright eyes and tight skin: my father was to describe it.

'I'd say—why bother yourself to be so regular about it? He'll understand. It's half-way across the blooming county.' He abominates bad language now, my father: and loves saying 'blooming': he rounds his mouth to say 'bloom' and seems to blow out his lips as if hoping they'll turn to petals. And words like 'county': he was coming into my mother's inheritance and mine with red nose and battered trilby hat. "Tell him," I'd say—though I knew you'd guess, Edward, I always thought that to myself. I'd say to myself, "He's too clever to miss it. He'll have guessed." But she wouldn't have it, you know, your mother: when her mind is made up it's made up and that's her mind. But, dear me, Edward'—he used the full name as if it were a title I held—'that trip would ruin her. She'd come back—get in here and sit down on that chair—*that* chair, *her* chair, and just— well she couldn't speak for a start: she'd be, you know—she'd, well sometimes now, sometimes she'd cry: not *cry*, just weeping tears, you know, not able to stop herself. Or shake. Or—Oh! A terrible state. It would take her the next day to get over it and by then she'd be planning on her next trip. Nothing would stop her getting at you, lad: you could bank on that.'

If, occasionally, I tried to persuade her that once a week was enough, she would go silent and be hurt: and take no notice.

'You don't mean that,' she would say. Or, 'I know your mind better than you do.'

And I would accept these old blows out of respect for her death. 'Each one kills the thing he loves'— games like that kept me some distance from the reality of her tyranny which had once been so welcomed, so hard had I sucked at it, so sweet and full her flood. When I turned away, the lack hurt, like someone peeling back the shaven skin of my skull and, on the quivering nerves and cells, briskly rubbing with sandpaper. Strenuous liberty.

'Mind you,' she said to the doctor, 'you have a beautiful setting for the people. They can look at the fells.'

We all three looked at the hills which guarded the nearby Lake as these two guarded me.

'Yes,' he replied. 'I'm surprised this area hasn't more places of recuperation and convalescence. Mountains do seem to help people. Like the sea.'

'Switzerland's the place for these homes really, though, isn't it?' she asked.

'Yes. But they have the sun there.'

'And the snow. We don't have that much snow here.'

'The two don't appear to cancel each other out, it seems. But the sun always wins.'

'Not here.' She shivered, suddenly, rather violently. I put my arm around her shoulders and she yielded to me.

'We'd better walk on,' I said. 'Perhaps back into the building.'

'No, no. Once we start moving I'll be all right.'

'Can I walk with you a little way if you're going in that direction? I must pop back into the house. The light was so clear: it made everything seem so clean out here: I *had* to come.'

'It *is* clean air,' said my mother, walking with over-determined firmness.

We walked, the three of us, she in the middle, through

the barren azalea grove and up the slope to the path which was lined with silver birch trees.

'You said "building" a moment ago,' the doctor looked at me inquisitively. 'I always call it the "house". Most people do.'

'It must have been a lovely house when it was lived in.' My mother's response was an interruption: she sensed a liaison which she could not share and so feared and so attempted to sever. Both the doctor and I shared a smile and in that his question was also answered.

Again guessing that another move had been made without including her, my mother dragged the trail yet further away.

'You once told me who used to live here, Teddy. You told me all about them. Some important people. Not titled people but very high-up. Who *were* they, Teddy?'

And I explained; with dismissive dutifulness and filial piety, I explained. The world was full of people I could not react to: I could not react to Geoffrey in the coffee bar that morning—to react, to have allowed the working out of the meaning of whatever relationship we might have, to do that would be to do too much: I was thus diminished before him and similarly before my father, though occasionally I *did* try to ruffle the complacent sentimentality, pour troubled waters on the oil. If I could step down for them I could bow down for her. So I explained what she already knew about the High-Ups and she kept the illusion of control and was soothed.

'I'll come and say good-bye before I go, doctor. I'll come to your office but if you're not there I won't wait.'

'Oh, in case, then, goodbye Mrs Johnson.'

We stood and watched him trot up the steps and into the house: like children staring after a train.

'I always go to see him before I leave,' she said,

76

hoping to contain a threat in a mystery and transmit it through an irreproachable habit.

But I would not let her get away with it.

'So he tells me,' I said, and in silence we walked on the gravel at the front of the house and onto the big lawn.

Even though it was only mid-afternoon the hills were in black shadow. Cut out against the blue winter sky. And the sun watering through the beginnings of a ground mist. It was cold.

'I like that nurse,' said my mother. 'Nurse White. She reminds me of Sheila. Sheila never got in contact again, did she?' The deliberate tone; always deliberate.

'Mother, you know the answer: you have asked and received a thousand times: I'll give you all your illusions for as long as I can and you need them: on principle and out of regard for you whom once I must have loved before it turned from the light to the grave. I'll do that. I'll play at being your son. But, Christ in heaven, patience is another thing.'

'No,' I said.

'Nor Eileen?'

'No.'

'I knew they hadn't.' She waited for her lead to come out of the rhythm of our steps: like an actress timing a line she listened, and then: 'You could always write to one of them,' she said. 'Now—I know that makes you mad. But it doesn't *really* make you mad. I know you take notice of what I say—afterwards.'

The alternative is to beat her down. It seems to be my only alternative. I've employed it. I employed it even when I was at school: her power had given me the knowledge of it when I needed it. I would contradict her, not nastily, not arbitrarily. Take, for example, that she knows that it doesn't *really* make me mad: her mind is full of that. That she knows me because she has made me and whatever I protest I do, I am being

77

false to a *real* self which she alone knows: and it is the *true* self because she knows the truth better than I do because she decided on the truth.

Once I would have taken that attitude of hers to pieces: patiently or angrily depending on the circumstances.

Then, however, she did nothing but agree with me. She lost all that pecking curiosity and perky righteousness which characterizes her and delights me: she went into a full retreat, and the only way I could make contact would have been to have followed her further and further into herself, cutting myself off from my resources, my supply lines, delivering myself to her in another way. Perhaps I ought to have done that and discovered the consequences. But the time for that passed and now we must play our parts: the old parts.

'*Beat* her down,' I wrote. She would not stop for persuasion.

'If you wrote to one of them you might be surprised. Maybe one of them's just waiting for a letter from you ... I think I liked Eileen best: she would have made a good wife for you. And maybe she's just waiting for that letter. Funnier things have happened; you read in the papers. Funnier things than that. She was very nice, wasn't she? A really *sensible* young woman.'

I did not reply and we went down the path which circled the lawn. In summer they played croquet there, I'd been told. A gardener—like my father in aspect as well as occupation—was squatted staring at roseless thorns.

'I know you don't like rich people but houses like this must have been beautiful,' she said.

She is forever presenting me with inflexible statements which might or might not be accurate There is no arguing with them.

'The man who owned this place, who built this place, was a friend of the Lake Poets,' I said.

I knew that she would be pleased, though her knowledge of the Lake Poets was scanty: she had never read them. But it was her son who was bringing her gifts: and she knew how to receive them. I never had a better audience than my mother.

'Make sure they look after that eye of yours,' she said when she left. 'It must be very aggravating.'

4

The sunglasses were slippery on my nose which was oily with sweat. Nor were the sunglasses exactly the right size. I had looked at myself in the little shaving mirror they provided for the purpose and, as always when I wear sunglasses, thought of the Riviera and Bandits. I remember the thought and I remember the reassurance I had gained from the fact that it *was* my usual reaction. I had smiled at myself in the mirror and then noticed how white my skin was; and my face ached when I smiled.

Out of the cavern coolness of the shop I went, and at another shop bought another cake, either forgetting that I had already supplied myself with one, or seeking relief in a transaction and relationship I'd proved equal to.

I placed the apple cake carefully on top of the pineapple cake. This buying of cakes, bachelor-like and old-fashioned, was an affectation. Over the years I'd gradually sought out and found my particular English type—my social type—and I kept it up. I knew it for the farce it was, I think, most of the time, and would cultivate that slight stoop only to throw back my shoulders once alone on the Heath. Since I have changed so much and am looking elsewhere or want to grow rather than to appropriate, it is difficult for me to imagine my former self accurately. I can see a timid-looking, cautious, sex-starved apprehensive man with a carrier-bag standing at the pavement edge ready to cross; I can pretend that all this is just a mask over glutinous fantasies which secretly stoked the Real Life of Edward Alfred Johnson as he stood at the pavement edge waiting to cross. Knowing more, I can tell you that the nervous and bewildered air was in fact his last skin, his last self; threatening him was the invasion when the cars and the lorries and the drills began their mid-day work up Perrin's Court, the V.C.10 flying low, the dustcart which was still in the High Street and now appeared in its death agony, gorging on the bins which came from a back alley which was the supply line to about half a dozen restaurants—when all this ceaseless noise, these strangers and attacks would burst through that membrane of self which quivered, nervous and bewildered, and gave and rippled with fear but did not yet break or split.

I want to help him. From this distance. I want to step back into the past and take him across that road he dare not cross. My present confidence would enable me to dart and dodge through the traffic: Ted, at that time, could not move without safe space well cleared on either side: right, left and right again. The rules were clear. Behind his sunglasses he cried a little: ordinary frustration mixing with and relieving the pressure to run which could not be acceded to for fear of where he would stop; or not stop at all.

There are those times when time itself will not move, it seems, will not go on, or only so slowly as to be the turning rack.

I want to help him. I could dart and dodge through the traffic. I have my balance now. Since being here I've learned to play tennis. The doctor taught me. I'm not very good but I can play. We run hard on the red asphalt court, occasionally stopping to talk. I could not play at all until he taught me. That is what happens to all boys who have no talent: I was no good at rugby but I could have been *some* good, not *very* good but *some* good. They don't teach you unless you are already talented like Rod: unless you are half-way there, already graceful as Rod is. Masses of people cannot play these games at all: those who need most help; those who need most help are generally given least.

He was not sure, at the pavement, that he could co-ordinate his crossing with the speeds and distances of the cars. You may think it rather stupid of me to speak of 'him': but I see so clearly, the carrier-bag swaying gently on two fingers, the string already having made a red mark, sunglasses slipping down the bridge of the nose, too tight behind the ears, rasping against the skin; helplessly there, he is far away. Nor do I want to bring myself back to him by using 'I': 'I', this present 'I', I wish to be done with all that; with all him.

An aeroplane goes over here as I write: aeroplanes sometimes blocked my head like migraine for days on end when I taught and lived in south west London; an aeroplane went over Ted very low as he stood on that bloodless pavement, that wide pavement in front of the flower shop—before him the pageant of clothes, behind him the blooms. A V.C.10—as beautiful a thing as has been made this century—-no wonder (I tried to digress, I wanted to stray) no wonder sculpture retreats to design sketches, to promises before that fulfillment, that graceful, glittering thing: passing and re-passing it seemed, like the dustcart's sound which would never stop: I could not imagine a world without it. . . .

It was the 'tough', the youth who got me across the road. He beckoned. It could be to no one else but me. He waved me to come to him; and I went.

He came very close to me and I saw on his forehead little beads of sweat, but so heavy and still that I could not understand it until I guessed that the grease from his hair had mixed with his perspiration: but wouldn't that be oil and water? Maybe sweat was more than water (or less) and grease was less than oil (or more) and so their repellant properties were annulled.

82

I did think of that as he talked. Oil and water. Because I dared not look in his eyes and yet was compelled to look at his face. I concentrated on that beaded fringe of sweaty grease.

'You know Wendy, Wendy Fletcher. Right?' (The girl who lived upstairs.)

'Yes. Do you . . . ?'

'She's a nurse. Right?'

'Oh. Yes, she. . . .'

'Leave her alone.'

'Sorry?'

'That's all. Leave her alone. Or you'll get it. See?'

'I. . . .'

'Don't talk to me back. Leave her alone. And I'm watching you.'

'Look, you've made . . . you must be . . . you. . . .'

'Yes?'

He paused. I tried again—but the rocks were crashing on the waves of my mind: real, actual, present fear of him had given me an external unease which seemed to remind my internal enemy of its power and encourage it to re-engage. And, looking back, I think that if I *had* been able to explain, or been composed enough to take him back to my flat and show him the layout, then he would not have continued to believe, or dropped his suspicion that Wendy and I were living and sleeping together. For, like the skinhead on the milk float earlier (and I kept seeing *his* face again—superimposing it on the 'tough's' face as my father's face had unnervingly become composed into Geoffrey's), he had rapidly run out of such a public and unintimate anger. 'You, you, you.' I could hardly even shape the words: my throat seemed suddenly lined with the dust from the street, and scaled with condensed exhaust fumes; I stumbled so as not to fall but had to stop and be silent.

'I'm warning you,' he said. 'Keep away from her. That's all. I'll say no more. But keep off. Right? Right?'

I might have nodded, for *his* head bobbed, as if in a nod, from charity or out of some habit of obedience, or perhaps to warn me of a butt. His greasy brow inclined to me for a moment and he walked away. Up the street, shoulders swinging: and sweat was on my brow, cold; smooth as oil.

* * * *

Tagon Street. My street. I turned to face what had left me; for the street became the image of the 'thug', the 'tough'—I never knew his name and I need the crudeness of the description to help define both of us. He had reminded me of the hard boys in the dance hall when I'd taken Lizzie; and Tagon Street was where they might once have lived. He had shown me how open I was to violence—no longer was the book an invisible cloak as at school, as since: I was feeling violently and I attracted what I felt. Yet he had not touched me and walked away after the warning.

Tagon Street was battered; staggering through dereliction to the beginnings of a new life; it too was no immediate menace, but I turned and saw myself assaulted by all the vicious, the violent and the poor, the distressed, the unfortunate, the oppressed, the lonely, the new-dead and the half-alive; they seemed to come out of the houses arms outstretched for offerings or fists clenched to pummel—and, as with that single man who had just threatened me, real fear and possible fears became mixed with unimaginable fears.

Yet I had to be steady: what else was there to do? Comically I counted in fractions. It was then, I think, that I first thought of a very ordinary image, a very straightforward analogy but one which was helpful. Certainly, its inception and imagining spanned the time between the man's departure and my arrival outside my house, having run, in fantasy, a gauntlet set up by all the back-street terrors of gangster films and childhood realities. The image was of a small boat in a massive ocean with nothing in sight, no land, no cloud, no bird, no fish breaking the surface, no sound; and I alone on it; I who by this time was shaking with fear at the idea of being alone. There were two alternatives: one was to give in, to dive overboard and sink, to lie back and be burnt by the sun—to give up: the other was to steer a course and hold to it, knowing that to change now would be even worse than the minimally useful gesture of steering a course. And all I could do that day was to hold to the day. To keep alive in it. To move through it and not give up, not go under. So, as I went down the street, past the imaginary people coming out of houses which were flaking and crumbling in my mind much worse than in reality, I saw this small boat, rather like a raft; a white sail, blue, hard blue everywhere and silence: I held that in my mind and arrived at the house.

As I went in I heard Mr Snell call out to me and knew that he wanted to be consoled about his recently kicked car but pretended not to hear. I was exhausted and my legs shook as I went up the stairs. I lay down in the bathroom—the quietest room—lay next to the bath and slept a little. The first blessing of the day.

*   *   *   *

On Hampstead Heath I concentrated on Cumberland. I was feeling better after the sleep: so much better that in the relief I dismissed all the morning as a freak time. I was feeling better. The shocks to my eye and my mind began to lessen. Those hours since getting up had been not only long in themselves—vast—but they had allowed no thought of the future. Standing on the pavement I had truly seen no possibility of doing anything else: sitting in the coffee place, I'd felt no strength to get up and leave it. The effect that this suspension of belief in your own continuity has, is terrifying and violently exhausting. But I had slept on the bathroom floor, and when I woke up, felt calmer. I drank a glass of water to clear my throat; bathed my eye which was also calmer, not flickering though still swollen; took a couple of apples as all the midday meal I was capable of, and went out into the heat of that August Saturday. Tagon Street was shaded by its own buildings and the shade was soothing.

In the distance—when I was on the Heath—in the distance I heard the Fair, and again was reassured as the sound of this August Bank Holiday London Fair was cheerful—in daytime, at a distance—its engines somehow rhythmic and the music from the records a more happy orchestration of twentieth-century sounds.

To be quite sure of my steadiness, and to nourish it, I chose to walk away from the fair—in the direction of Highgate ponds—and tried to think of Cumberland. Rather like that nervous virgin on her wedding night who was told to close her eyes and think of England. I tried to remember as many encouraging facts and times as I could. Yet—how odd this is—it is *now* that I can feel myself *then:* it is this present which can feed that. As if Dunne's theories of time had come true and his 'past, present and future' continuum had been proved right: for I can think of very little *he* might have thought of then as he walked across the Heath; very little, that is, which would give him the comfort he sought and needed. Much that has happened since can do it.

Yet I could have thought of the sound of the fair and how I used to spy on it when it came to our town. Being no daredevil, I did not spend vagabond hours there like Rod. Nor had I the money for more than two goes on the speedway: and even those two turns had to be carefully taken when no one from school was looking, otherwise I'd be forced to play up my tentative hold on the wooden toy bike and appear the fool. Rod could sit on it backwards, stand on it, straddle two, move around from machine to machine imitating the men who took the money. I couldn't do anything like that.

Lizzie could. We'd gone down to Morecambe, four of us in a car. I hired it and the boy friend of Lizzie's best girl friend drove it. He had no licence. They had opened up part of the fair for the Christmas holiday and Lizzie was looked over, optically fondled and stripped, by the fair boys and some others who bumped past—and how she deserved it! Even now I cannot think of her without the clear memory of longing! And though she was herself excited and vulnerable to suggestion and wanting to be wild, she had stayed with me; she had not humiliated me; she had favoured me. I had kept her.

There is the sort of trouble you think you will never get out of. When I was eight I climbed on our roof—this before the retreat, before the spectacles and the stoop—and spent a summer afternoon looking down on to our street and over other steep, tiled roofs. Saw chimney pots and possible places for hiding a hoard of jewels; worked out routes through the town—roofways. When I turned to go back down I slid. On the sun-shined tiles I slid and my body—lazy from the lying down and half asleep—my body skidded inside my clothes and did nothing to prevent the slide to the gutter edge and below that a drop onto the concrete pavement. At the edge itself, my sweating palms stuck to the tiles and stopped me. And then I waited. I said, 'If I get out of this I'll believe in God, Jesus Christ and the Holy Ghost. I'll never be bad, I'll never dirty my clothes; I'll always help mammy. I'll do all I should.' Even now I remember how long I stayed there: how many hours those few minutes were: how many days and months of my past seem as winks of an eye compared with those few minutes, palm-stuck to that roof.

That was the sort of trouble you think you will never get out of. All the way back to the roof-peak, backward-crabbing: and then just as slowly forwards down the other side—all the way, the prayers and the gape of time.

That Saturday morning had been such trouble—except it was so much more alarming than anything I'd known, and so distressing that perhaps a parallel from childhood diminishes it: except that childhood's fears are large: but not as vast as an adult's fears. Little children *do* suffer: men suffer more. The comparison was to point out the *quality* of the trouble in its connection with time. Time did stop, as they always said it could.

So I breathed in deeply and stepped out briskly and thought of good times, past times, on the Heath.

A gang of skinheads swept past me like a company of destitute commandos; but I was no longer under attack from myself and they sniffed no war in me.

Despite the holiday crowd, the Heath still bore its regulars: each segment of the day had regulars, different each from each as if the one orange was made up of multi-coloured slices. The unexpected spurt of juice between my teeth as I bit an apple! The tension of *that;* how good it tasted and the way I bit it, so clumsily did my jaws work, so painful were they from the fear of the morning. I remember I bit the inside of my cheek and it bled a little but I tickled the stub of torn skin with the tip of my tongue and tasted the blood gratefully.

Had I been open to violence it would have been scented by those skinheads. They were sent to try me. I was cured, I thought.

Then, at the beginning of the hard times, for that day was the beginning of months of hard times, when I walked in mind-blindness came the first illusion; I thought it was all over. There had been a jolt of the brain, there had been a crash, a fall, but it was over:

there would be damage and bruises, but it was all over. To say I walked briskly—I could have run down to Highgate ponds, past the silver-haired bent-backed Austrian doctor (my fantasy) trotting in his blue satin shorts, past the middle-class women with their middle-class accents and massive aristocratic dogs, I raced without paying my toll to the gleam-eyed beggar in his torn black coat who gave me a shiver of a future self as he held out the hand for a shilling—past them all to the preoccupied daddies playing at being their sons with the yachts in the ponds, to the tireless lengths of leg striding out still here and the recognizable faces prepared to be boarded and to all the company of this Heathen host: I could have run—so soon did walking in nature revive memories of walks when indeed I had been untroubled.

No fractions; no raft at sea; no child in the throat.

So as I walked away from the fair and away from Tagon Street and the High Street, I cried again; a second time; out of relief and the memory of happiness. Yet it was the imagined past, not Nature, which was the real cure. We must do without Nature. 'Never saw I, never felt a calm so deep.' Written of London.

I had the luck, good or bad, to be brought up surrounded, imprisoned by natural beauty. Now, as I write this, here in Cumberland itself, I have only to go across to the window to see the fells, the bare hillsides with only the stone walls to show a man's work like snail-tracks at this distance: such hills all the more appealing to our present sentiments for so easily appearing to shrug men off. And I must consider carefully whether the Heath, that speck of natural scenery, could evoke such as this: but need not think for long, knowing that a scent can evoke a woman, a sentence, a city, a taste, a whole period of life. So as I strode, threatening to run, as I went along the Heath I let the yellow green grass, those walls so brittle-seeming with the lichened stones, the restful edges of the hills and the plashy feelings disturbed with succulent life by the depth of beauty in the Cumbrian landscape; let that run through my mind's eye as this bare tonsure of London, or this crown of the city, made a way and a space for ease.

*   *   *   *

At Kenwood House, which I'd taken care to approach through the bottom woods so as to have the advantage of seeing it high before me, at this most elegant bequest to the nation, I took tea—not in the stables where, with a continuing comprehension of status, the cafeteria had been constructed—but in the garden. Formerly, no doubt, the vegetable garden—but a garden: walled, whitened and hot.

There I'd first re-met Rod. That is, I'd—that is, *he'd* —we'd met again. We hadn't seen each other since—I was about to say—'since University', but I *mean,* since vacations. I remember that reunion clearly.

*   *   *   *

It was in January but, again, as again and again in this story, the sun was out, the sky blue, the weather brilliant and I'd walked all the way around the Heath, rather like a vicar stepping out his parish—or is it only bishops who beat their bounds now?—and I had convinced myself that the move would be successful, that my apprehensions were Childish, that I would soon Make Friends, that Tagon Street was Just Right—a simile for the whole of London with Irish labourers and West Indian families of six in two rooms at one end and advertising executives at the other—that I *didn't* miss the cosiness of Twickenham, that ... even then, from the very beginning, there was the flaw.

I only went out into the garden because inside, the cafeteria was crowded out by a group of old people who'd come, as I saw later on a card in the window of their coach, from Islington—a neighbouring borough. There was no free seat but even though I wandered through the tables looking for one, I would only have taken it on principle: for they depressed me. They were too like too many old people I know and too like my father in a few years' time. They were all small—all: then every one of them had probably been underfed when children; all were very poor and so neatly dressed, such polish on the shoes and starch in the collar, such care for the lace on the blouse and specklessness of the velvet hat: perhaps I was a little tired after the walk; certainly I was already becoming disturbed, or already allowing my past self to be confronted by what I wanted to live by in the present; but there was so much attention to such little details in the over-large clothes (and still the envies there and the loves, still—even a stranger could see—still the affections led them on, the great themes mercilessly playing themselves out still under the shrunken skin), that I was in danger of either weeping or instantly changing my life and becoming a social worker. Either course would have been useless and self-indulgent: what *had* to be done was to find a free seat and speak if spoken to, or even, if tact and circumstances were in a good combination, begin the conversation and so market the day. But there was no seat.

I saw Rod as soon as I came out. I was shy. With his television programme and his novels he was quite a figure now—in *my* pantheon anyway and I did not want to impose on him. But he waved: he 'beckoned' (even in generosity he is the sort of man whose self-awareness cannot escape the accusation levelled against affectation), and I obeyed: I was glad to. I was grateful.

Perhaps I underestimate myself but it was nice of Rod to be so helpful at that meeting. He had obviously wished to be alone: he looked strained—that appealing charm which came over so clearly on television was masked by an altogether more adult, more knowing expression. He was not 'like' himself—and, to confirm this, no one recognized him throughout that afternoon. Later, he developed a theory about being 'open' and 'closed' to being recognized, claiming that he could be recognized or not at will. So, that afternoon, no one recognized him because he was under strain and did not look his public self. Thinking of him now, through the filter of my own trouble at that other time, I would guess that he was attempting to digest a belly-full of difficulties; to keep going as the television personality *and* the novelist, and also, as I was to learn, a man of many affairs, brought him problems whose entanglements could be disturbing. But he welcomed me. He almost 'interviewed' me for the first few minutes. I could have been on one of his programmes.

I particularly remember one section of the conversation because in it, I believe, was raised our new friendship. 'So. You're setting up shop,' he said: he liked to summarize what you'd said, but he'd do it in such a way as to bring you firmly into his sphere; as if by describing you to yourself he could influence your attitude towards him, make it more pliable. 'You've come out of the suburbs and into this mini-city we have up here. You've got your flat, you've got your job, you're establishing yourself on that magazine. Oh yes, I read it: I know you'd all hate my stuff (if you ever read it) but I'm your most masochistic addict. You've cut off from the imitation-of-home-roots in the suburbs and you're on your own. You're part of what's really happening, Ted. Good.'

'I thought you were going to say "welcome aboard".'
'Did you?'

'You do make it sound as if I'm getting into a position for something momentous. I'm not, you know. I've just changed my address, that's all. To be nearer my new job.'

'Come on, Ted. Let's pretend that the past gives us some sort of intimacy with each other. You hope your life'll change. You want it to, don't you?'

Now I realize that he was thinking aloud: he was talking about himself and politely transferring it to me because he was talking to me. The strain which was on him at that time was too severe to allow my interruption to be of any real account. He had discovered not only a willing ear, but also someone he could pretend was an alter ego.

'Everybody hopes his life will change.'

'Do they hell. Most people crap themselves if they have to change.'

'What's so marvellous about changing?'

'Nothing,' he said emphatically, 'except that we're stuck with it and we've got to find a style for it.'

'Most people we were at school with are stuck with marriage.'

'I've been married.'

'I know.' I explained further. 'It says so on your book-jacket.'

'Does it mention the divorce? Forget it. Sometimes I get paranoiac about my private life. And it's so unimportant anyway. They'll be open now. Let's go and have one. I didn't know you'd read my book-jackets.'

'I've read the books.'

'And? No. *Don't* say. *Please*. Even if you like them. Let's have a drink and keep bumping into each other in this cultural reservation. No Lit. Crit.'

As we got up to leave, the old people came out of the cafeteria and Rod winced: he turned the other way, unable to bear to look, which so pointed up my own earlier reaction that I was forced to look again, to check the dismissive pity of my former self and discover the irony in some glances, the grace, the indomitable bitterness. We walked through them, so much taller than they were; taller by two generations of carnage.

I recalled it all as I sipped my tea on that August Saturday afternoon; and ate my second apple, looking at a notice which said that patrons were not allowed to consume their own food on the premises. And I thought of Rod-of-the-morning, trotting down the street after the successful actor; and of his invitation. He had taken me up, Rod, in a small way, without distressing himself too much. That day must have been a low point for him—he's never been as friendly or open since. We drank quite a bit that evening and talked a lot—about the school and the town. His two novels have been set in the town and he loves to gossip about it—not as one 'gathering material'—but because, he claims, it is in some way a family for him. But I transfer to *him* what belongs to *me*. For if it is bound up with one of us it is with me: he finds it a convenient back-drop for his rather discursive and 'thoughtful' novels in which he disguises his fiction, often, as a documentary record. Both of us enjoy talking about it and that night the freshness of the meeting and its unexpectedness loosened our recollections: we got drunk on the past. As we drank more and talked more, he lost the strain, he lost the tenseness and the beer flushed his face; the charm returned; people recognized him.

That first afternoon with Rod decided the direction of a number of other matters. I believe I would not have stayed in Hampstead had he not been there as an example to be envied, in fantasy to be emulated and also to be enjoyed as a friend—though I was soon to discover that he spread his friendship wide and thin. But that afternoon, that wintry day with the two of us in the walled garden and the old people from Islington —I used that a good deal as a touchstone.

*　　*　　*　　*

The thought of Rod, then, and the knowledge that I

had something with which to seal off the day—his party —and, through drink, see me through the night; and the sun, the grace of Kenwood and the placidity of all those people in deck chairs on the lawn down to the lake where in the evening the orchestra would play, the steady commonsense of the leisured saunter which most people adopted as they came out of the wood and up to the house, the cautious tread of that quiet pleasure which appears exclusively middle-class English—all this diluted the concentration of anxieties, and I decided to take advantage of my mood—or, though it now seems foolish, even comical, to test it, by going to the fair. There was time before Eileen came to tea.

I know the Heath well and chose a 'back' way across it. As I came nearer and heard the music I began to be afraid; to realize that what had happened in the morning *could* recur. But in some essential part of myself I was committed to this Fair. If I did *not* go to it, I would be even more vulnerable. If I turned away from this reality there was my own waiting to rise up against me. As if a black cloud has passed over the sun on that cloudless day, I with leisure and time, appearing perfectly normal, walked towards the holocaust of noise and movement which the Bank Holiday Fair had suddenly become. Even as I went between the two ponds and up to the car park of cinders where it was mounted —even then I began to shiver.

Out of nowhere this fear had come. Out of nowhere. I had nothing to fight it with. What could match it?

The first thing I saw was the Big Wheel; and heard young voices screaming.

5

For a paragraph or two I must pause to tell you something which seems to me to have an essential bearing on this account.

Three days ago, I finished the previous chapter and saw Ted walking to that fair and knew what was in store for him. He fights back there, but as the day closes so it closes in on him and he suffers a good deal more: how he endures it, how he responds to it—the nerve involved in his reaction—all this is to tell. But, I thought, how can you want to know more? What, you may ask—as I have been asking myself over these last three days—what is especially interesting nowadays about a privileged young man having a breakdown/breakthrough/change of consciousness? Even if he does try to qualify his privilege by pleading ordinariness and takes the trouble to make associations between what is inside his head and what happened outside—and makes a story of it as well. The tough will turn up again, of course, and Geoffrey and you must have guessed that Rod's party, for example, should be important as well as being packed with the sort of people we're always seeing or listening to or reading about. But though the party might be important for the story, what importance has the story?

A week ago I would have replied unhesitatingly that any man's life can be made important; it depends on the quality of the imagination which presents it.

Yet I saw, over this weekend, some of the less lucky people here. The doctor must think I'm very much stronger to invite me to help him. They are very short-staffed and I was glad to be of use. Already I feel guilty about taking anyone's time here: there *is* no equation; there *is* no justice in sickness or in health. From time to time the fact of an equation being impossible gives you pause. As I have been given with the coincidence of this story and my life.

There are people here in serious distress, whose courage and helplessness are beyond my description: and to make more than the statement that they are here would be an intrusion. A greater liberty is now about to be taken, for, briefly, how can I write my story after spending these two mornings with the doctor helping in simple ways? Their misfortune makes mine appear trivial, such dwelling on my storms in the brain when I am surrounded by minds truly and perhaps everlastingly shipwrecked. On those days I write nothing.

Yet now I see that I can write the story because I have recognized the needs of those met on that day, as clearly as I see the needs of these patients here. Other times, other habits; the same wants. And when you have seen and tried to sympathize, then degrees of distress are another, perhaps even a secondary, matter.

Writing thus becomes an act of faith as well as a demonstration of egotism: a belief in your own place in the world—that it is given to one as to all. This I had to face on those days; and plant the idea of acceptance where it would grow. And so, even if what I can tell you are small, unsensational matters which many of you are too strong to consider important or too intelligent to dwell on for long. No! There is no call for such grovelling. He went up the cindered path, I, Ted, and into the fair and heard the screams from the Big Wheel and saw Wendy with a girl friend of hers: she waved and whispered to her friend; telling her, I did not doubt, that I was her neighbouring virgin from downstairs.

*　　*　　*　　*

I. It was here the turning point, I think, for better and for worse; here that at last that day I began to break out of the 'I' which until then had enclosed me like an eggshell and set loose its malign contents on itself, myself, without any chance of my breaking out. At last I had the relief of seeing other people as they might be.

What began it was the sight of the 'tough'. For as I made for Wendy and her friend he came into my sight-line, standing just behind them, leaning on the upright of a circular wooden stall which was devoted to a lottery for immense dolls. He was glaring at me, glaring with all the force he could summon into it, warning me to stop, to swerve, to go away. But as I came nearer his expression changed, I thought, and became first afraid, as if he knew the hopelessness of his own postition, was well aware of it without having to take on the misery of additional competition, and then the expression became as of a man pleading, 'Please leave her for me, please give me a chance,' and my heart beat more firmly and more steadily than it had done all day. For I understood his helplessness and so felt less defeated by my own; was sorry for him and so felt less sorry for myself. I imagined his lonely pursuits and useless vigils: I guessed now that at one time Wendy must have nursed him. (In three or four minutes time she was to tell me just this; that he had been in her ward for eight months with smashed-up legs after a motor-bike crash: but it is important that it be noted I had already guessed that. I had already got out of myself by myself.) I sensed his muddled frustration that she who had rested her breasts on his chest as she bent over him to soothe him, who had helped lift him out of the bed and come to share many common jokes and private nuances with him, that this loving nurse and mother and friend and ideal mistress should turn her back on him and bury her face in pink candy floss while he leaned beside a row of fat oversize blonde-haired blue-eyed baby dolls: there could be no equation in his mind.

More, as I came nearer to her and so to him. I could imagine his home—and strangely, as always in these situations, be confident that what I was thinking was not an invention but the truth—could feel the neglect in the clumsy scrupulousness of his best white shirt open at the neck and the comb jutting out of his breast pocket; in the white skin, see the anger which had settled on him and been sealed by his own glut of rage. There was a family in our street when I went to school—a family of thirteen children—and many of the boys now had the look of this man, and they, too, when I return home, regard me as an enemy. It was with them, as with him, that my affectation of studiousness, my crimpings and crampings of manner and style—all were revealed for the minor deviations they were; for in *their* eyes, I was lucky and safe and that was that. And the 'tough', the lover of Wendy; already he saw his case as hopeless before the advantages which seem to have struck him as being as obvious as caste differences. Strange for me to appear superior to anyone at all.

So by a small leap I left myself for a few moments—perhaps spurred on by fear or perhaps using imagination as superstitiously as a charm against possible danger; no matter. In those same few moments I beat down the fright which was turning, rising inside me. I decided—*determined* to fight it, for if I collapsed, let it at least be on the Big Wheel or in a Dodgem Car.

Wendy pushed the candy floss into my face. 'Have a bite, stranger.'

I chewed off the sticky cotton wool, sucked it, and felt it shrink into minute pellets of coarse sugar.

'This is Susan. You must have seen Susan. She comes to see me on Sundays.'

I nodded; almost bowed. Wendy was over-excited. The noise, the striking primary colours, the whizzing and banging, the lambent threats of the pack of skin-heads and the strolling pairs of police, the crowd's mixture of Cockney and smart Hampstead—all this added to the thrill she obviously got from the attentions of the man who wanted her.

She put her arm through mine: I must have reacted a little nervously.

'Don't worry. You'll be safe with me.' She addressed a theatrical wink to Susan. 'It's your money I want not your ball-bearings' Then she patted me on the stomach, on the flap of my unnecessary jacket, 'Hang on to them,' she said, 'you'll be able to trade them in one of these days. Collectors' items.' The over-emphasis some-how leavened the lewdness of tone and insinuation and you had to smile at her. 'Right. Take us on the Ghost Train. We need a guard.'

She was a big girl and when she pulled me in the direction of the Ghost Train, I was jerked off balance: she steadied me in her arms and muttered, rapidly and a little proudly:

'See that bloke—the one beside the dolls. White shirt. See?' I touched her back to indicate that I did: we could have been mistaken for lovers standing there as if hugging each other: she had me in a tight grip and was not going to let go until I had been told what I had already guessed.

'He's been hanging about all day. He was in my ward once but the silly bugger's fallen for me. I've said hello but that isn't enough! Stay with us for a bit: I'll pretend you're my boyfriend—that'll finish him.' She stood back and beamed at her ingenuity. Then, to reassert herself, added, 'It would finish you an' all, mate, if you took me on. Ha ha ha. So to speak.'

Her speech was a mixture of imitation cockney, imitation Hollywood, imitation Able Seaman and unmistakeable hockey-sticks.

'Right. No standing and starin'—let's take a look at that little ole Ghost Train.'

'No,' I said, 'let me take you onto the Speedway.'

'Now don't get frisky, matey. Susan 'ere's been told you're a reg'lar gent—not one of these Hell's Angels.' The thought that I might be a Hell's Angel so surprised Wendy that she shouted with laughter and 'collapsed' into Susan's arms, smearing her friend's face with the last bits of candy floss.

On the Speedway where the two girls instantly began to sing the words of the song played at full volume— 'Creedence Clearwater Revival' were the group; I remember Susan screeching the name into my ear: I'd asked her where she came from but no matter. I chose a motor-bike: so did Susan. Wendy sat on a streamlined duck.

Her 'lover' came, hovered, and then, after a kindly but detached smile from Wendy which brought a flush to his cheeks, sat over-negligently and rather glumly on a motor-bike nearby: stretching out his feet so that they rested on the seat of another machine.

The man who came to collect the fares asked him to take his feet off it. We were all watching him, politely screening our attention by various common devices but certainly watching him and, aware of this, he refused: crossed his legs and settled them more firmly on the seat. And flicked the man his shilling—not quite neatly enough so that the man had to step back to make sure of catching it; he stumbled and plomped down on the seat of another motor-bike. Wendy laughed and it was a bouquet and curtain call for her shadow who then stretched out most possessively and by his whole attitude clearly challenged attack over which his opponent now hesitated. The machine slid into action; all the fares were not collected, the man made it obvious—again without words, the attitude alone communicated it—that he was called away by duty but would go reluctantly and not forget.

Nor did he. As it gathered speed he came back. With a friend, to stand on the rising and dipping boards which formed the clearway between the traffic of the wooden machines and the gaudy booth at the centre where sat the controller of cash and speed and sound. So a network of glances was set up: between the two men and the 'tough': between himself and Wendy and himself and myself: between myself and Susan and eventually myself and the two men; and finally between the two men and Wendy and Susan; and Susan and Wendy and the two men. They were obviously out to hustle him but did not and I would suggest that this was possibly because they thought that he and I were together; that Wendy and Susan were our two girls; that there'd been some internal argument among the four of us. That explanation would be easy to find evidence for in the interchanging glances and reaction to glances: it would diminish the seriousness of the challenge offered by Wendy's lover (we all strut before those we want to admire us) or at least lessen its relevance to *them*. Finally, as one of the ironies worth pointing up, if I were his friend then the sides would be equal—two against two: he looked very capable and I, in my dark glasses, deliberately urging myself on to go through the middle of this storm, with my jacket open and my 'labourer's' body forced into a position of some poise by the speed of the roundabout and the rather determinedly graceful attitude a motor-bike encourages you to, I, too, might have seemed capable.

I clearly remember realizing this possibility at the time. It seemed then that my attempt to think of him had made him make me think of him so that he, unconsciously, was helping me who, consciously, was concerned only to help myself.

They left him alone.

'*Now* the Ghost Train!' Wendy would not be deflected. 'Come on, Susan. Prepare To Meet Thy Doom! Sweet? Ted! Do—you—want—a—treacle—toffee?'

'Thanks.'

The Ghost Train.

The Whip.

The Big Wheel—and there I saw across the Heath where I'd walked and up to the street where I lived and knew that I was escaping. But why should it be only an escape? I was taking it on. I remembered a few months previously when the uncertainties and fears had begun, I remembered then that I had deliberately walked around Hampstead Heath at night: not a great test of nerve, you might think, but for someone like myself brought up in a small town, this Heath, this land open to all comers at all hours, unpatrolled, unlit, the place for voyeurs and scavengers and ravers late at night, murmuring with threats, it seemed, and sucking to itself the frustrations of that massive, nocturnal city as by day it soothed the irritations of urban life. It is no place for someone to walk around alone at night if they are nervous. *Most* nervous and the more unhappy because I was just beginning to see the connections, just realizing that somehow I was both strong enough and weak enough for my past to confront my present and demand that accommodations be made or the structure pulled down and rebuilt. Tentatively and anxiously, I'd walked around it. I felt much worse afterwards. Though I believed (faith again) I believed that in some essential but not directly useful way, I'd helped myself. Similarly at the fair. Now, at a distance of seven months, when I look back on it, I know I was right to stay and right to play the part of the gormless rustic intellectual, right to walk into the middle of the noise and the things and the

103

sphere of a person who could do me harm. But at the time I also knew that I was building up more images, more sounds which were going to attack me later: I was not only putting off the evil moment, I was giving it more power.

The Lottery.

The Hoop-la.

The Rifle 'Range'. Wendy won a garden dwarf.

Darts. Throwing darts at playing cards which were pinned to the floor. I won a pair of cut-glass ashtrays. I gave one each to the girls.

'*You're* not as green as you're cabbage-looking,' said Wendy, suspiciously. 'That's what you say up North, isn't it? The way they speak? We had a lorry driver in last week from Newcastle—you'd think he'd been born in Hungary the sense you could make of him. "Hinnie" this and "Hinnie" that. The minute you went near his bed you knew, though! By gum! That's another thing you say, isn't it? By gum! He had hands like rattlesnakes.'

To keep up my part—my caricature (of which I'd grown rather fond; and quite pleased with the way I played—over-played it), I seized this moment: 'What *do* you mean? What did he use his hands for?'

'Collapse' of Wendy on Susan's shoulder.

At one stage she said:

'Are those just sunglasses or your own specs tinted dark?'

'Sunglasses.'

'So you don't really need specs.'

'Oh yes. But I need sunglasses more.'

She reached out and snatched them away from my face.

'Your poor eye,' said Susan, *much* less breezy than her friend, 'what did you do to it?'

'You tell me . . .' I was, I hoped, jocular: without the sunglasses' protection, my eye began to smart. It

104

had been quiet so far during the afternoon. I wanted the sunglasses back without any fuss but when I reached out for them, Wendy waved them above her head, out of reach. Such a simple evasion almost made me weep in exasperation.

'Now let Nursey have a peek-a-boo,' she said and beckoned my head forward: it followed her finger; her finger went to the eye and, joined by the thumb, prodded the swollen area. 'Probably cold in it,' she said. 'Or a nerve that's decided to pop up and take a look around. How long has it been like that?'

'Since this morning.'

'Have you got anything for it?'

'I bathed it in hot water.'

'That's as good as anything. It'll go. I *thought* there must be a reason for those sunglasses.' She sounded quite cross about it; as if I'd cheated her by appearing to have a new aspect—only for her to discover it as an easily explained adjunct to the old.

'Put your sunspecs back on, sucker. And let's hit the trail. Lulu's back in town.'

She'd decided to call him Lulu. She wouldn't tell me his real name though I asked her several times. Still he followed us around, managing to look both bored and dangerous. I wanted to invite him across and tried to argue Wendy into accepting this.

'There's no argument—no!' she said. 'I'd never be able to get rid of him—you don't know what they're like, some of these patients,' her hands deep in the pockets of her home-made mini, she kicked out gloomily at the cinders. 'They want to marry you, to take you round the world, to give you presents; it's absolute hell!'

'Still,' said Susan rather mischievously, 'he *has* taken the trouble to find out where you live.'

'Find out! *Him!* Sister would give him my address. She'd fall for anything. They just ask her for something and she does it. Some of them are like that, you know,' she added, rather desperately, 'they treat these bloody patients like Royalty.'

And from the depths of her melancholy, her true character emerged: a well-brought-up English middle-class girl with pony lessons and an ample suburban background. Money around. Having a 'fling' before back to the lawn roots and happy families with 'old thingy' who was doing 'quite well'. The tough, the fair, Tagon Street, no doubt myself and perhaps shy Susan were part of the 'fling'.

'I have to go,' I said, 'I have to get back.'

'Well we're coming too, baby. There's no joy for Wendy with Lulu on the prowl.'

'Just be decent to him, and he'll go away.'

'You don't know glue, Sonny Jim.' She laughed. 'Glue pots are sticky things.'

'I feel sorry for him,' said Susan.

'You *would!*'

Wendy glanced around. She *was* attractive—had that tremble of enjoyment and expectation about her which could easily infatuate any man. To her present hopeful attendant she was obviously Cleopatra herself, confident, ravishing, obviously one who would love making love and yet proud. (Did he like that about her? For she treated him like a base petitioner. If he hated it why then did he not either challenge her or go away? He must have loved it. Which left all his hatred available for me.)

We were on the East Heath road beside the row of stalls which followed the trees down to the Green and the buses. Here the fair turned into a market and the number of Indians selling goods together with the general mêlée on this expansive suburban highway, usually reserved for fast cars and sauntering pedestrians, somehow disturbed me. Yet another change: perhaps the fair went on forever: I would find it in my flat.

I wanted to get back to my flat. Eileen was coming

and there were preparations to be made, but, more important, I wanted to carry away the strength I ought to have gained by daring the machines to throw me and whirl me and tumble me about: I wanted to take it into my flat without losing the feeling of it so that I could imitate it when it drained away, as it would; so that I could use it to take me through the time that must be tentative and tender with Eileen whom I *could* come to love.

'If we saunter down towards the Green and then belt up Heathurst Road and cut into Keats Grove and back down we might lose him.'

'He knows where you live,' I said.

'I've got a lock on my door, baby,' said Wendy. 'Remember? I need one with sex-mad monsters like you around.' She took my arm. 'March on, Casanova, and keep those hands out of them thar pockets.'

He let us get ahead before following. Politely. Unchangingly.

6

'The first thing I noticed that I remember—and I've sat and thought hard about this; I've tried to picture it all as it happened—was that he had been crying. He said it was only his eye watering and even slipped his sunglasses down his nose so that I could see the nasty lump on it but he had definitely been crying. I was sure. It made me feel shaky. I can't remember seeing a man cry—not someone I cared for. I wanted to turn away and let him wipe it off his face.

'He was definitely thinner. I'd seen him last at the technical college when I'd gone back there one afternoon at the end of the summer term. He had lost a noticeable amount of weight since then.

'And his room was very dusty which was most unusual because he was so "particular" as they say. I noticed beside the chair I sat in, there was a rickety little old-fashioned table with a glass ornament on it; he'd told me once it was a tear-glass which was appropriate, and the table was covered with dust, like a tablecloth.

'If you want an overall first impression, as far as I can remember, I would say there was definitely a *peculiar* feeling about the place. After all there was a fair on nearby. It was a lovely hot day—I know *how* hot because (you said you wanted to know "as much as I could put down"!) I'd decided *not* to wear a slip even though the dress I had was sort of gauzy and, against the light, "see-thru". But somehow his room seemed more damp than cool—I can't put my finger on it exactly—"peculiar's" best. And he looked washed out.

He was letting himself go. In some ways I should have welcomed it: usually he looked so, I don't know, *too* tidy, *too* much dressed like he had been years ago, always wearing something that wouldn't offend his parents or anybody, but somehow wearing it awkwardly and sort of grinning at you if he noticed you'd noticed it. His attitudes made me uneasy in things like that because when you brought it up he denied that it existed: he wasn't as tidy and that was nice. But he was strained: maybe he'd—well, I know what happened since—but then I might have thought it to do with his notes and those lectures; he used to write them over and over again. He always worked far too hard.

'I'm trying to "talk" it on to the paper as you said instead of writing an essay about it. I've just read what I've written, though, and it seems too gossipy for me. Still, I'll do it your way. Anything to help.

'So those were my impressions at the *beginning* of my visit on that afternoon. It was a strange occasion in more ways than one and I recall a good deal about it for more than one reason.'

Eileen wrote an enormously long letter to the doctor. My mother—I can only presume it was her—had given her the address of this place. She wrote to me. I did not reply. She wrote to the doctor asking if she could help. He consulted me and replied suggesting she put down her impressions of that day: he told her he would show the letter to me, which might have inhibited someone less conscientious than Eileen. She may, of course, have seized on that to insert a direct communication to me.

I lied earlier on when I said I'd cut off entirely from the 'women of the winter coats'. Eileen *had* been the last of them and we *had* split up the previous Christmas. But we'd seen each other now and then over the months—sometimes slept together. She had been an assistant lecturer in Physics at the college but her real interest had always been in social work and she had left the previous year to work for an organization like Shelter—housing the London homeless. Oddly and, in some way incongruously, this work, full of stress and unhappy experiences, had smoothed her out. I am led to this by her comments on my own appearance. Those very short mini-dresses suit most women because of the attraction of a run of thigh: Eileen who had taken to them late and reluctantly, looked stunning. Her legs were very good: no longer housed in woollen tights and anchored in suede boots of ungainly style, the legs emerged and the rest followed. She'd cut her hair short. I had not seen her for a month or so—maybe it was that gap which made me aware of how attractive a woman she could be: or perhaps in my state her attractiveness was heightened.

I knew Eileen would stay with me if I asked her. Or rather, I wanted to be that certain.

She came in. That meant that Geoffrey or Harold had let her in. I had heard a door click on the landing and I knew that Wendy had used the pretence of coming down to answer the bell in order to spy on me. I should never have taken that place. Promiscuity of any sort irritates me now, violently. I hated Geoffrey's knowing that someone was with me: I hated Wendy's 'assessing' Eileen up in her crow's-nested bloody flat! She put on her Loud Ones—I remember that. Their rhythm was background to our conversation.

When Eileen sat down and crossed her legs I saw the dab of vaginal knicker—white. Usually, this was the visual button which set the count down for take-off. I don't remember the history of that particular reaction but I do recall, clearly, that dab of white—it reminded me of a bandage.

*   *   *   *

110

'What did we talk about? Well, he hadn't a great deal to say at first: in fact he was so quiet that I thought he was just "eyeing" me up and wanted to get into bed. I suppose you'll want to know all about the sex angle!

'It embarrassed him, I think—not doing it so much as getting round to it in the first place. Usually there would be this *dead* silence: whatever you said would fall really *dead*. Then—to be honest about it, I'm sure Ted won't mind—it was *me* who normally suggested it —you know—"It's about time we went to bed" or something. And I *hated* suggesting it. But he was definitely even more worried about it than I was. We would usually get undressed as fast as we could, never looking at each other and be between cold sheets in about half a minute flat. It wasn't so much, let's say, mad passion that got us there so quickly, though: more like just—embarrassment.

'I can't write about what actually went on between us. He was very nice. Sometimes he frightened me a bit because he *is* very strong—or can be: but mostly it was fine. I'm sure we could have got on better if we'd talked about it or joked about it or even admitted to each other that we were curious about it: he was against all that.

'But it wasn't *that* kind of a silence. I got up quite soon and made the tea. He'd bought some cake especially for it and I was touched by that. He was full of unexpected things like that—and pineapple cake, he'd got, I'm sure, because I once said it was my favourite.

'I didn't like that flat of his I'm afraid and I probably went to make the tea to be on my own and get over the Anti-feelings it gave me. He'd made it look too "classy" for my liking—all those paintings and ornaments and that stupid furniture he was so pleased about. I didn't mind his books—they were *part* of him—but all the rest was just the leftovers of a way of life which had nothing to do with him. His modern paintings were fine—we

111

both knew the people who'd done them and they were authentic. I assume you know about his possessions: he must have told you. It annoyed me very much the way he went on about them as if they mattered. I thought he was better than that.

'When I brought the tea back in, he had not moved; I mean that exactly as I write it. He had not moved one inch. That convinced me my first instinct had been right: he had been upset and was still upset and needed help. I thought talk would help.

'Little things, silly things. I ate two slices of pineapple cake thinking he would understand that I was ready to help him from that.'

*　　*　　*　　*

You see, as soon as she came in—because I knew she would help if asked, because of the relief, all the fear which had been beaten away at the fair. God, I thought, let it not begin again; but there was the lurch in my throat, the kick—Jesus I can't put print to use for this: I feel like raking my pen down this page, tearing it with my nails, soaking it in the substance of that torrent which I had no power to stem. I wanted her to know this flood was between us.

I could not tell her. Not only did I want her to understand it without my saying so—*that* would be proof of love: the certain proof I wanted—but it was too difficult to talk without breaking down. As long as I held it in, let the storm go through my head—so slowly, so slowly, so slowly—then I could be intact. Words connected me—with her, with their own history: I did not want to connect—no connection, none. She had to discover my grief and embrace it: for myself I could only hold on.

Yet, how—how absurdly strange! There was this tea to be got through. Cups to be picked up and put down;

pineapple cake to be eaten, carefully, so that the juice did not dribble. Moreover, as our last meeting had been in irritation and I'd invited her to tea to preserve the cordial courtesy we both considered worthwhile at that time, there was attention to be paid to the politeness enjoined on us by that. To have ignored it would have been an over-forceful declaration of renewed interest or a revelation of helplessness.

I concentrated my gaze on that dab of white. Between thighs lightly brown. Succulent flesh, she had, the more tender for being so long shrouded. The white dab like a paw. Threatening to grip and claw, I thought, to tear and disrupt the even flesh. And always the roar of the gorge in the mind.

*   *   *   *

'I talked and he answered. That was it, really. I can't bring to mind a great deal except one point which *did* strike me, and I've thought of it a lot since. I had something to do with his state of mind, I'm certain now. Though *I* thought of it at the time as a victory for me.

'I told him about some of the cases we were working on. One in particular—a woman with five children who was being evicted for the third time in a year. The case is still with us. Her eldest boy had run off several times and the last time had lived for three months by scrounging cash, raiding milk machines and sleeping at night in the back of parked lorries. He was nine. Three of the children had eczema. The woman was pregnant again. And the unbelievable thing was that, living in *one* room as they did, sharing a kitchen with three other similar families and the house having a single lavatory for eighteen people—she was as cheerful as anybody I had ever met in my life. She wasn't thirty: she had varicose veins and a wrecked figure; her "fourth", as she called him, had "made her have all her teeth out"

113

and the false ones made her gums sore—and she was as sunny as sunny can be. It was horrible, somehow.

'At one time, I'm certain, Ted would have said that this was just a form of hysteria—something like that: but no—this time he just nodded and said he could understand it. I couldn't.

'Previously, you see, that would definitely have been more than enough for Ted. I think out of a kind of unable-to-bear-it-any-more feeling, and a general guiltiness that a lot of people get when you tell them about what is happening to approximately half a million people in London—he would have brought out all his boring old arguments against Do-gooders.

'But he didn't. Even when I went on to talk about Richard Tupper, who runs our outfit and *is* a bit hard to take—you must have read his stuff—he didn't get angry. He *did*, however, say a remarkable thing. He said he thought that people doing what I did definitely *needed* to be personally selfish and vain and conceited, to defend themselves against being swamped. People like him, he said, could not do such work because in fact they could not cope: they could not accommodate so many in such great distress: they had difficulties enough coping with themselves. I'm going on longer than he did. He said it very succinctly. Yes. There *was* such a thing as integrity, he said: and it had many meanings. The simplest was "keeping yourself together". And it was the most important. Do-gooders should realize that selfishness is a real occupational hazard and just accept it.

'I was very struck by that.'

*   *   *   *

I remember her talking about it. The people came into my head. The twilight people, poor, poor, people that my Self would normally exclude: caught in the swirl of my sick mind that day: the rats and the running walls. Oh! never a nightmare like Eileen's plain facts, nor horror like the statistics she raised and let fall: drowning all of them, in me they drowned: like the past which made me wince, like my fantasy of Tagon Street and that man who followed Wendy: listen to the world how it wails and the laughter of the secure is indeed hysterical in these valleys of death, echoing, echoing.

I must show you her—this woman—Eileen. In as much as I had loved since Lizzie, it was her I loved. It was not glorious.

*   *   *   *

She cleared away the tea things and when she was out of the room this second time, I got up. I returned the notes to my desk. The blood must physically have run out of my head. I was dizzy and had to hold on to the desk.

She came back in.

'Are you all right, Ted?' She came around me and looked intently at me—but only for a second, afraid to intrude or fearing the intimate consequences: I don't know which. She took a few steps away.

'Are you sure? Would you like an aspirin? Where *are* your aspirins? Why don't you—sit, sit down.' She picked up a cushion of the seat. I watched her rather carefully—somehow, wearily, able to detach observation from other faculties. She banged it rather gracelessly and dust rose. 'Maybe you've a touch of this 'flu that's around. A lot of people have it for a day or two. Why don't you sit down? This chair's clean.'

I nodded. Having been stupid enough to let a slip show I would have to win back the ground or let everything go. If I forced my distress on her or pointed it out to her then she would deal with it superbly and mistake the admissions for a declaration. So might I, later, at

115

some stage. Things would be irrevocably shifted by the act. And she could have called me to it: her cry would have found a true echo, most likely: most liked of them all, she was.

But she padded on the surface. I saw it, that day, so clearly. I was afraid my need would hurt her.

She was standing. I wanted to see that dab of white, that paw: that paw would move me if not to a bed then to a chair—for that bandaged, hygienic, lacy paw drew up so many associations that I would be deflected from this inner greed which sucked in all my will.

Then she turned and looked at me 'seriously'. I could not bear the attitude. Though she was *indeed* 'serious', her stance was such as to make her scrutiny appear affected. How unfair! But there it is. She was 'weighing me up' in some Serious quarter of her mind. I was, perhaps, In Trouble. I could not bear to be A Problem. You may consider this mere vanity but in fact it was to preserve some possibility of real affection between us: if I played The Problem and she The Solution we would be stuck in roles. They might, they could well, fit us, suit us: they could cause to come together a coupling which might have happened anyway. Yet I suspected that I would not be able to emerge as I wanted to after her pity: such new skin as I might be growing would be rubbed away in the care and nursing. I knew, truly, that day what I was not, and about the raft going in a single direction. My course was to reach the end of the day on my own. Nobody's problem. Just one day. None. Except, Oh how I wanted this! Except if becalmed by a real love.

She came towards me, her arms opening; to hold or hug me. If only one of us had been sure which it was!

'I'm all right. Really. Just let me stand on my own for a minute. Get my balance ... that's it, see. ... Could you —*could* you get me a glass of water?'

She went to the kitchen and I used the interval to go

over to the chair and sit down. After giving me the water she hovered over me, brooding over me, shading me from the sun. I sipped a little and gave her back the glass, thus obliging her to move away.

'Why don't we go to the fair?' she suggested; as cheerfully as she could under what were becoming 'the circumstances' to both of us.

'I've been.'

'Who with?'

'Alone.'

'Take me.'

'It was too noisy.'

'For your head. I'm sorry. You *must* have that 24-hour 'flu. Or your eye's acting up. Is it throbbing? These things usually do. Mine went like that once and it felt as if there was a midge in it or—'

'What?'

'A midge, you know. Or a bug—some sort of flea inside it, jumping about. It got on my nerves. Have you put anything on it?'

'Yes.'

'It'll go soon.'

Oh Christ! If only I could propose something. If only I could find the key and turn it so unobtrusively that she would not notice yet be wound up to tick away for the next half hour or so. How long would 'tea' last? The white dab. The paw. I thought of a new child bursting through that white gauze; struggling out under the cool summer dress between the succulent pink-brown thighs. The child would be blue and crumpled; slimy with blood and water, contorted and wanting breath to cry: soon to be slapped into its first call on the world—a howl. The punctured little shoulders wriggled between Eileen's smooth, unwrinkled thighs. The image, as I remember, calmed me down. I might even have taken the opportunity to dab my weeping eye.

I asked her and prompted her about her job. I wanted

117

her to talk on what both of us knew, so that she could feel easy and I could think of something else. She was so sweet—plainly there in her spartan summer tunic—bra, pants, dress and sandals, freshly bathed, fresh-faced, free in conscience and hope—that I felt my manipulating of her would be forgiven were she to notice it. She would welcome the chance to understand.

Eventually, she began once more to talk about her job. Like many people in England now, she had been educated longer than her merely academic interest wanted or warranted. What she had found by 'staying on' reading Social Sciences, and then by 'staying on again' to start a thesis and then by 'lecturing a bit, part-time'—was not scholarship but a church. It is tempting to use the word 'faith' but that would be too strong: she would have welcomed a faith, sometimes she seemed to yearn for a faith, she admired men who Believed, Stood Out, were Principled and so on—but her nature was not so passionate as to be unable to compromise, and, like most of the others she rested in a Church. This was built not out of bricks and mortar; rather Marx and Humanism, though Marx was almost a memory by now; later, more synthetic materialists had taken his place. Her assumptions were that the society she lived in was Capitalist and Wrong; that the Individual had to do All He Could to Help; that to work towards rehabilitating people, for example, was undoubtedly the finest possible way to spend a life; and that fashion, society and riches were matters of indifference, though pop, personal appearance and taste were questions of some moment. She was modest, but, how shameful it is to admit this—on that day I thought her predictable.

Why should it be such an irritation to be predictable? Before I got into this state or changed as I have done, I would have defended Predictability most vehemently —saying it was the metronome of Integrity and Reliability and Consistency in a character and so on and on, which, in some ways, I still believe. But now I see the shadows more clearly than the forms, the mist is more apparent than the long, detailed perspective; there is ambiguity where all was clear and everything can be reversed. Perhaps one day I will be able to get back to solids, to certainties, to an appreciation of such Predictability: at the moment it is incomprehensible and even inimical: and at that time the cracks were opening into which dropped the seed of this moment. Or perhaps I envy those who are predictable as the lame must envy the whole.

However that might be, her words could have been spoken by scores of others I had met and taught. They were to do with 'the System' and 'the Bureaucrats' and the Welfare and the Middle Classes and so on: with little variation she could have been talking about half a dozen causes or even half a dozen different subjects Possibly it was this which irritated me: disturbed by the demands for recognition which my self was making so fiercely, I could not bear such blanket descriptions of others: everyone was unique and even the most helpful attempt to group, to categorize, to classify, to generalize on lives was then to be resisted. I myself had talked like her: as the system taught us all childhood assent, so, later, our dissent was uniform. She I could have loved was as trapped as I had been and the more she described what I had been, the less I dared welcome her. I could not go back. She reverted to her job.

How it absorbed her! It was work, hobby, interest and could be all her conversation without a pause; the news, television plays, books, films, chat about friends, all would be sucked into the Job.

She was good.

I tried to recall what I had thought of before the fair. To recapture that mood on the Heath when I had imagined myself to be through it all, to be free from it all. If I could think of what had held my mind together—for that was the strange distress I then had—there was not a thought in my mind. Eileen's words came on relentlessly—the woman had refused Welfare Accommodation and 'done a flit' to another borough; it was her son's birthday and her husband had stolen the money she'd saved for his present—facts came and came at me but stopped outside the brain: inside was dry, empty, the bottom of the sea, a sea which had long been drained, still the stench, the dead things, the landscape reminding—but nothing stirred. I felt only sensations were substantial; I felt that nothing need ever again stir. Eileen would talk. I saw her gentle face and sweet, pale, unpainted lips talking as if obediently: and I would listen. I saw myself there, upright in the wing arm-chair. I saw all the objects in the room, one after one —those before my smoked gaze for I did not turn my head: I heard the roar of a car, the ripped nerve of a motor-bike, the wash of main-street traffic: I smelt the dust and the plucked odours of a street in that hot late afternoon, and I was an object with no wish even to die; remembering, indeed, that I had sometimes wished to die, to surrender to the force of the fear—or perhaps I had no memory either.

I could have been a mollusc on the floor of this drained dead sea. I remember that most clearly and it is true. I could have been a stone.

Time passed. The spaces between minutes can indeed be very long. An immense time passed in those few minutes while Eileen told tales of unhappiness, injustice and despair. Gradually came the resolution: I must hold on to her.

How mean I have been about her! She was brave to go to rat-run basements, damp and full of bitterness and apathy: she was marvellous to be so cool in circumstances so hysterically dreadful: so she looked well, but her lack of paint, of pointing, of glamour, of seductive

120

airs—that was admirable and even lovable, wasn't it? Eileen, Eileen, this is what I wanted to come out—but perhaps your goodness makes me so aware of my weakness or so envious of your strength that I can only be critical when I should be full of love.

I wanted to hold on to her. But neither to throw myself on her charity, nor profess a love of her which I could certainly not be sure of then. She, too, was uncertain though for different reasons.

I wanted her to interpret her feelings: to articulate mine for me.

'The thing is,' she was saying, 'the authorities just won't let out the facts. I mean, this report on the Homeless in London which is being done now. I know one of the researchers on it—Peter Bomford; he was at Durham with me—funny, his middle initial is C—for Churchill; anyway he's hinted at those figures—well, more than hinted but it's more than his job's worth! She smiled at this friendly treachery; a gift for her. 'They're about the same as ours, you see. In half the London boroughs fewer than 27 per cent of homeless families are offered Welfare Accommodation. That means that four out of five homeless families are permanently on the move from one shack to another in London now. And other figures—like they say that few parents are separated from their children whereas *we* know that most are. The bureaucratic bastards just tell lies. The point is, *we've* said it again and again and they've got to the stage where we're sort of part of the scenery, and they can take no notice.' She was cheerful about that. To me it seemed no great boast. 'If a Commission said it, that would be different. But—just watch—they won't let it out, this report. Already, Peter says, they're altering this bit and holding back on that—you know, limiting the definition of 'homeless' still further—that kind of thing. The point is that in the end the people who do the enquiry, however nice and that they are, they're

121

the same sort of middle class person as those who run the councils and the welfare or the big charities or the government departments. And of course *these* people give evidence and the Commission believes them because it's like talking to like. And nobody wants a fuss. And after all this urban homelessness is world-wide and probably better dealt with in London than anywhere else and so on and so forth. They can always cover up by saying it's better here than abroad. The English Establishment always uses that one.'

I give you every bit as much detail as she gave me: it's weight was crushing. I wanted her to stop. She was, I acknowledged it, talking about something far more important than my troubles but it is an indication of the degree of self-concern I had that I wanted her to stop. Fear makes a man conservative.

She paused.

'They'—my throat was swollen, I was sure, thickening visibly, I knew—'they help to kill the thing they love, the Establishment; England, that is. Those who own it are the men who would do it to death.' I could talk only through the paraphrase of someone else's words —but into them I tried to project a certain lightness, to put a stop to her talk in a way which both showed an understanding of it and a route out of it. She could have recognized the quotation, or asked about it: above all she could have sensed the mood and stopped.

'That's right,' she said eagerly, brightly, encouraging me, 'that's exactly what'll happen here. Peter told me that they're frightened they'll have a sensation on their hands even though they're dealing with sensational material, and so what do they expect?' She made a clumsy dramatic gesture; of hopelessness. 'Apart from anything else, the government is definitely less likely to act on a revolutionary report than on a mildly reformist one.'

'So it might pay to lie.'

122

'How?' She followed into my reaction, most happy to have me authoritative.

'At least . . . at least something would be done.' Stop.

'Hm! *We* can do *some*thing. But the point is that the capitalist system is less and less geared to minorities.'

'. . . Luxury goods are enjoyed by a minority. . . .' Please . . . Stop. 'That's different. Aha! That's part of my point. You see, you have this minority: but the system is geared—low-geared but better than 100 years ago—to the majority it can use. You see? In affluent times that's a real majority: even, perhaps, in difficult times, but at all times it ignores the minorities who are *not* useful. It's crude utilitarianism, really. Now take those in Welfare Accommodation and "the children in child care". . . .'

I was helpless before her enthusiasm and totally unable to rise to it. My effort now went into prompting her to continue so that at least there would be sound to fill the space; and a sound I welcomed, her voice, reassurance, contact, a life.

But I could not keep it up and soon there was silence.

I let it grow. Eileen, too, I would swear it, she also knew the silence to be positive, a last or even an only hope.

It could have been the silence which precedes the decision of unsure people that they will begin the moves towards going to bed with each other. As it grew I recognized the similarity and encouraged myself to think that it was *not* 'the same as' but the real thing. I wanted to want to make love to her.

When talking in her platform-intimate style, Eileen had been graced through her excitement: despite the mechanical attitudes it was as if the skin actually glowed —that sweet, docile skin—and its illumination sparked the rest of her, tinted her rather dull hair, shaped the slightly unyielding form, pointed up what was attractive in her. And I could forget my discomfort at her in some way scooping personal benefit from those who suffered, the feeling that there was mockery somewhere in her becoming more attractive the more she did of this unhappy work. But when she stood, and patted down the hem of her dress which had creased under her and rose as she did, rumpling to the top of her thighs, and when she took those two or three steps towards me, the illusion was gone : she was like a learner on a tight-rope; or rather one who would never learn. So that when she sat on my knee and then, thinking to be even more intimate, jolted or half slithered off it onto the floor to rest her head against my legs, I was already losing. I stroked her very short hair: or rather my fingers pushed against it and the tough skin at the finger-joints felt the drag of these short tufts of hair—thick, it was, and threatening to be curly.

I cleared my throat as if to say something; hoping indeed that the action would remind me that things could be said. But I had nothing to say.

How pathetic a figure I was! That is not excusing myself or insuring myself. Appreciate straightforward self-contempt. The *luck* to have Eileen there that day! Perhaps, indeed, I had allowed myself to—change, break whatever—that day (and there was, in my case, *some* element of control still: enough to have held back a day or two or undergone it earlier, I think) only *because* I knew Eileen was coming. I knew that she was safe, she was reliable, she was the nearest to a sensible love and a positive life I had had with a woman and there seemed then no earthly reason why anyone in any way 'better' should ever come along. Nor since, though I may have managed to temper my fantasies and my ambitions, have I met anyone remotely as 'good'—for me: as attractive a combination of talents and characteristics as I could reasonably aspire to be joined with—and how pathetic that, too! In the marketing of emotions never trust any-one, not even a former self—no one.

For all this is rearing high before the obstacle before me : the shame I feel to tell you what followed. And— to be fair to myself—the retrospective tenderness I feel for Eileen makes it scarcely bearable. What matters awkwardness when there was so much goodwill? Why such a cruel demand for empathy when she was so sweetly good-hearted? I made faults out of her virtues, to distract attention from my own: but they widened in the attempt, as they must. Yet on that day, I could not see her otherwise.

She looked up—up at me and most certainly smiled. Pulling herself round on to her knees—I remember how sharply her elbows dug into my thighs—she reached up to cradle my face or cup it in her hands. Her touch made me panic—it was like a switch flicked on tense skin: I jerked my head away and my sunglasses caught her hand: they went askew on my nose. Still smiling, she took them off and, still looking intently at me, at my eye obscured now by this growth of nervous flesh, she folded them neatly and placed them at a distance.

I was afraid. She wanted to make love and I did not. She thought I did and I did not want to hurt her by objecting to a notion I had definitely encouraged—to be loved—though not in this direct way. I was afraid because her hands on me would make me scream. I was certain of that.

Still smiling, like a nurse to a patient, smiling sweetly, she undid the buttons of my shirt from throat to waist and playfully tugged at the top of my trousers and I could say nothing. I knew that she interpreted my looking away from her as shyness; just as she interpreted her own action as sensual. Trembling—for she was no lascivious lover, no heroine of the hardbacks who'll sink their teeth into a man's privates as keenly as they'll bite a peach—she twisted and fumbled with the catches which secured those trousers around my waist. Perhaps faint stirrings of farce rustled over the dead seas of my mind: they must have done. In one way I wanted to help her—just to get it over with—be done with her clumsy and incompetent attempts: in another I was trying to call up the courage to say stop; no; no.

She panted a little, with the frustration of what was just possibly a totally new experience and then there was a sigh of triumph as she opened the waist-band; rapidly she slid the zip down and then she laid her cheek against me and nuzzled there, while above her I struggled not to shout; not to kick.

It was all so unfair. On her. Unjust, and from her point of view, cruel. Yet from mine, who did not kick nor even scream, kind: and from then on I could at least abandon self-recrimination: for, though you, you too, can only smile, I thought that I had made a sacrifice. I had not screamed.

But could do no more.

Sat upright and tensed and could do no more.

Slowly her melting tenderness hardened. Her sense of self-consciousness woke up to the implication of her position: embarrassment began to illuminate her.

I had long ceased to stroke her hair. Indeed, it was only a sense of propriety which kept me from locking my hands together and putting them behind my neck as a neck-rest.

'Don't you want to?'

'No.' I was contrite but could not sound it: truly I was, and am, distressed at her situation and yet the articulation of that now as then seems to contradict it; it even contrives to be merely rueful. 'I'm sorry,' I continued, 'I want to—but I can't. It's—I must feel worse than I thought. I'm sorry. It *is* useless though.' I added that last sentence because though giving her my sympathy I wanted to cut off any possible return.

'Of course you want to.' Her words seemed to come from a great maternal distance: and her head, too, all the way down there, averted still, diminished.

126

'I *know* you do. It just takes time, that's all. Sometimes. You're too tense. You'll be all right soon.'

'No! No—I, there's no point, really, Eileen, I can't. Not today.'

Here I made the final plea. 'Not today'—and with those two words I was saying, 'Ask me *why*; not today—*think* of why it has been so different this afternoon—here is a cue—take it—a cue, a clue, a key, a plea' but the small, short struggle of manners was over with me back where I was. Alone.

'If that's how you feel—fine.' Bravely said, without rancour. She stood up and smacked her dress as if chastising it. 'Well.' She smiled again—but this time it was cheerful and perfect: not intimidatingly tender with that promise of possessiveness, nor Brave in the Face of Overwhelming Odds—just a decent grin at the general situation. I stood up—to kiss her—it was a chance.

She stepped back.

'Watch it,' she said, 'your pants'll be round your ankles. You'll trip.'

I re-zipped, re-buttoned and re-fastened myself and she went out to the kitchen.

I knew that I had to ask her directly now. I had to ask her to stay—as plainly as that. When she came in, as she did.

'Well, thanks for the tea—and the cake. It was lovely cake.'

'Are you off somewhere?'

'Yes. I said I'd meet this Peter I was telling you about. He lives somewhere round here—somewhere in Hampstead—Mount Vernon. Do you know where it is?'

'Yes. It's—up the High Street, across the lights and then up the Ramp on your left.'

'Thanks. Very clear.' She laughed. 'Don't look so sorry for yourself. It was a bit silly of me to get carried away.

Anyway—dab something on that eye of yours.'

She nodded. And turned. And left.

*   *   *   *

'I would never have gone if I had known. I suppose I
did know, really, but we had a sort of unsuccessful
attempt at love-making and that threw me. I just
wanted to get out after that. But there *was* something
about him that must have struck me because I phoned
him later that night and again in the middle of the next
morning but there was no reply.

'I lied to him and told him I had to see another man.
When I got outside his place I went and looked up
this friend as a matter of fact—just for something to
do. We talked a bit and went to the pictures. After
that we had a meal and then I went back to my place.
I hoped there would be a message saying he'd phoned
and there was. I phoned back but, as I say—he was out.

'There is something that makes me feel guilty looking back, that I didn't do more at the time. I recognized
he was ill but somehow he did not want help.'

When she wrote to me I was in no way able to
answer. Just before Christmas I received her last letter:
since then there has been nothing and I can only assume
that she has given me up or found someone else. I
am sore-hearted when I think of her with someone else:
even now I cannot call up the times we had together
though only now can I see that they could have been
good and happy times. I have not yet the strength,
though, to face that. Not yet.

*   *   *   *

The door bell rang.

Eileen could not have been gone for more than two

minutes: it was as if someone had been waiting to pounce.

The door bell rang once more.

I thought it was her. I stood still a while to let the thought of her invade me. Once more the bell rang.

I got up and went downstairs to answer the door. It was Mr Snell.

'If you've a minute,' he began, already turning to lead me down the steps. 'If you don't mind.' He was someone who was truly incapable of imagining that you might have a life of your own going on: he acknowledged the fact of it—sometimes—but it never occurred to him as being a real possibility.

'Sorry to disturb you: won't take a minute.' He was at the bottom of the steps now, bending down and looking at his car. 'Come and look at this.'

I was in no state to resist his bullying. Look at what? I went down the steps and put out my hand to steady myself.

'Feelin' a bit dicky, old man?' Mr Snell, if ever any man did, leered: but he was not one to pursue such intimacies indelicately. 'Now then—this mudguard.' Oh, most casually did the conspirator proceed: 'You saw the business this morning, I take it? Hm?'

I did not reply. I could not remember. The morning was another life. He made me realize that he took my silence to indicate consent. I concentrated on being coherent.

'There, you see—scraped and dented. No doubt at all to my mind. Feel it.' He stood back and waved me to his mudguard.

'I'm sorry,' I muttered. I remembered now: the milkman, the argument. The words were gulped into my mouth and seemed to cling to my palate: ejecting them was difficult; it was necessary to remember how to speak.

'I didn't see it.'

129

'Didn't see what?'

'The mudguard. Your ... accident.'

'When the guy kicked it!'

'When the guy kicked it?'

'When he kicked!'

The words threw themselves against the front of my head and I struggled to hold them back.

'Of course you did.'

I shook my head—but blushed.

'Of course you did!' He was trying not to be angry.

Then I added an unnecessary lie.

'You can't see—here that is—you can't see from my window.'

'Hm! Mind if I have a quick shuftie?'

He galloped up the steps and into the hall and I heard the staircase creak as he ran up into my room: my representation of myself so carefully arranged and so secretly maintained. I was lashed by his intrusion.

The window was thrust open.

'Of course you can see!' He beamed. 'Nice number you've got yourself up here. I'll leave this window open. Your room's as stuffy as a submarine. Ever been in a submarine?'

He didn't wait for my answer. I was still looking at the window when Snell came trotting down the stairs. My eyes went down to the window of his basement front room: the lace curtains snapped shut but I'd seen the frustration and fatigue in the young woman's expression. If he thought his wife would be impressed by all this, he was, as often I presume, mistaken.

'*You* saw it,' his voice was so ingratiating that I felt a physical cringe of distaste. In some way he must have noticed this, for he built on it by crossing close to me and taking my elbow. I cried out; not very loudly, but it was a cry.

'I only touched your elbow.' Poor Mr Snell: his life must have been based on the certainty of trouble: every-

130

thing else was temporary intermission.

'I—I've had, I've had an abscess there,' I said. 'You happened to touch it where it's still painful.'

Mr Snell was relieved and in that state made no claim on me as I left him and walked up the steps. 'I think I'll lie down.'

I had almost convinced myself that there had in fact been an abscess and held my arm stiffly.

'You're sure I can't help you.'

I shook my head and mimed a silent 'No'.

I went inside.

'See you about this other thing some other time,' he shouted after me.

Geoffrey stepped out of his door and took what I now thought of as my 'bad' arm in a very fierce grip. 'You don't help that old prick if you don't want to,' he said. 'Don't let him drag you into it. He deserves to have that bloody car swiped. We're having a party tonight. You're welcome if you like. And bring your boots. Remember—every stamp on our floor's a crack in that old bastard's ceiling. Take care.' He disappeared as abruptly as he'd arrived.

I went into the bathroom. I was grimy with sweat and I tried not to remember the morning's fear as I ran a tepid bath. The bathroom was supposed to be the quietest room in the house but on this hot and airless day sound seemed to stir the air to a ceaseless rumble which drove into my head. I shut the window and shut the door and sat on the edge of the bath, trying to imagine that the fall of the water was like a waterfall in Cumberland. Such a sound was balm: such a sound, like the sea and a sweet soft wind on the hills—those sounds restore you and lead you out of yourself: here, you must build a ditch around your mind and always have it fenced and manned.

I stopped the water, pulled off my clothes, and got into the bath before the fear could attack. I willed the image of the open raft before my mind's eye and tried to relax but could not. The rumble was in my head; as irremovable as an air bubble in a phial—no release but by breaking.

I got out of the bath and took two sleeping pills. I put my mouth to the tap to drink and wash them down. Then I took a third. The doctor at college had prescribed them for me the previous term when I'd been suffering from insomnia.

I got back into the bath and washed the third pill down with water I cupped in my hands from the bath. Then, still stiff and tense, I lay back.

I had not taken off my sunglasses.

Two things only now: I put the chain attached to the plug between my toes so that I could tug it out should I feel that I was falling asleep. When I *did* pull it out—when the water was cold and my skin was pimpled with the cold and my brain was like an independent weight within my skull—then I lay in the bath and as the water drained out it was as if my blood were being sucked away, as if I had opened my veins and the lifeblood was going out of me. I could see the bath full of blood and my skin whitening, whitening.

I did get out; I wrapped myself in some towels and either fainted or fell asleep.

The instant before sleep I 'saw' myself. I was bandaged from head to foot in white bandages. Stretched on a bed in an attic. Inside the bandages was liquid. My mother opened the door and this bandaged thing managed to get up—was drawn to its feet by her power—and went across to her. She drew it—me—outside the door on to a lighted landing and said, calmly, 'You killed your daughter, you know.'

7

I am back in my mother's house now—another home—writing this in the room in which I used to do my homework. Out of the window I look across the street to a row of terraced houses identical to my mother's: the same period as Tagon Street, but smaller houses and prettier, working-class-respectable, a bit of money spent on them recently. I am as shut in now as I was then.

I decided to leave the clinic on the day my mother failed to turn up for her visit. We have no telephone and so I sent a reply-paid telegram: the reply said 'Please don't worry stop. Will come tomorrow stop.' I could not ask her not to but the effect of coming on that bitter spring day, with the long waits for connections and the freezing draughts of country buses, took so much out of her that I was afraid to let her go back alone and accompanied her, stayed overnight, tried not to lose my temper at my father's sentimental solicitude which resulted in nothing but slyly amazed references to his own health and strength despite the years out of doors in all weathers and (inevitably) the request for a little bit of shopping to do so that he could pop in the Crown for his half of mild. His cheerfulness and look of comfort increases as my mother withdraws into illness: perhaps he has not guessed that she will die soon; perhaps that will upset him more than all three of us might think. But her illness is a relief for him, no doubt.

After that night I returned merely to collect my things. My time was almost up, anyway. I had come in on a voluntary basis and no one minded my going.

Before I left, I went a last time to the azalea grove. It would be pleasant to punctuate this leave-taking by a symbolic bloom or even a bursting bud—but the spring continued to be an extension of winter and the grove was bare of flowers. I went there because I had often gone there at important times—the place was my retreat, more 'mine' than my room or even the library in which I was the only regular reader. I have never seen the azaleas in bloom and that may indeed signify some of its attraction for me. I wanted to believe that an old life had died, that a new life was under the earth of my apparently lead self: that there would be growth, new and certain, as there would be in the azalea grove when I had gone.

* * * *

Let me clear up any confusions you might have about time. I have tried to make it clear but with action occurring in the present as well as in the past it becomes hard to follow and it is important that you know where you are. Obviously I hope that the way of writing that I have felt I *had* to adopt (I could never have got started if I hadn't begun by an act of confession) has brought some benefits to the story; coming into it and going out of it as appropriate and so enabling me to re-direct it, change pace and comment.

There is another point, by far the most important but the least easy to explain lucidly. I went back into the clinic during the Easter holiday deliberately in order to go through that August day again, to face up to that experience once more, expressly to see if I could not only endure it but examine it. A certain caution took me there: I might not be *that* strong. And while I have been writing it I have been reconstructing the moods, even re-experiencing the symptoms (like the eye) which I had then and trying to set up defences against their possible

134

(inevitable I would guess) recurrence. I would maintain, then, that this has not been therapy so much as reconstruction; or is that therapy? I am not afraid to admit that writing may be therapeutic: fiction, however, is something else as well.

What I am saying is that though the cool room I had does not much resemble a lion's den, a viper's nest or a pit of flame—it could have been all those to me if I had not discovered fiction. By writing this as fiction, imagining what I could not have known or cannot ever be sure of, I have been able to take the risk of meeting myself in ruins which I was afraid might precipitate further ruin.

However, I did have the security of that clinic. I do not have it now. I am in my bedroom. Next door my mother is in hers. She is asleep. It is late afternoon, the same time of day indeed as I have arrived at on that Saturday. I encourage the coincidence. The doctor has just been to see her and I have persuaded him not to take her into hospital, which she would loathe and fear. There is nothing to be done but to ease the pain and that can best be done here, in this terraced house she so bitterly and agonizingly resented and was ashamed of, this small brick box which, nevertheless, she made into a pretty place, with simple things and an implacable sense of 'good taste'. My father has moved into the spare room which is the size of a box-room but suits him very well because he can smoke at night there. When I am not about to lose my temper with him, I am half fellow-conspirator in his liberated pleasures: it is disgraceful that he should be blooming so obviously. Sometimes we smile and laugh at each other as we pass on the stairs: in the silence of her house it is strange and, in the end, perhaps merely another face of fear: let that be our excuse.

So the security of the clinic is gone. No more food-points like stations along the day. I make the meals here

135

—my mother ceased to protest after the first week or two. She still chides me for my care for her; but that is part of our conversation.

I promised you a timetable.

Most of this is set on the August Bank Holiday Saturday in 1969. Most of what has been written so far has been written in the Prospect Sanatorium in Cumberland—in April 1970 when I used the Easter break to come in here again as a voluntary inmate. Now it is May 1970. It is much more difficult to write at my mother's house.

Last October, Wendy wrote to my mother's address (we had given each other our 'home' addresses at one sensible juncture as a provision against just such an emergency) asking about my absence (to her, of course, unexplained), and commenting politely on the flat's emptiness. Eventually a boy friend of hers moved in there: he sends me twenty-five pounds a month which is useful and is willing to quit at a month's notice. I simply put out of my mind what he may be doing to the place; how he may be re-arranging my furniture; how he may be handling my small pieces of ornament—especially the Roman phial—what he may be doing with the books. I had a brief capitalist, property-owning panic about it but there is nothing at all I can do about it: the panic went: the place leaves me cold. I certainly have not yet the nerve to go back there, nor (now) the time to go back and clear things up. Besides which, as I keep saying and as I believe, I am changing; I am no longer the stuffed swot who was set on by his past in that place. I have new ways and will maybe go back there to try them; perhaps only there *can* they be tried: I think of returning.

Now when I remember my waking up in that bathroom. The *thing* I was. I seemed to curl inside it, to cringe away from the form that I had been given: as my ideas had been drummed into me so my body had been dropped on to me—perhaps it is possible to see it as a Trinity—Brain, Body and a feeling of a Self. In the good times, now, on the good days, these three are together whole, wholly, each feeding the other and, most importantly, neither the brain nor the body throttling the self: this is over simple but everyone who has known his Self to be threatened by what he has been given or what has been foisted on him will understand. For others, a trinity is a useful illustration; it occurs often enough (in various disguises) in those areas of life where people have directed most passion. Its value, at the very least as an illuminating guide, is high : by these analogies we live!

The *thing* I was. Near the beginning of this account, I apologized for suggesting that looking out of the window (after waking up) was like peeping over sand-bags in a trench. By implication it made great claims for my state of mind and, though I am anxious to ensure that I am not attempting to mislead you and am aware of what was involved in those trenches, in so far as an historical observer has access to awareness, yet on con-sideration I believe it wrong to have apologized. I called the analogy 'inappropriate' or said it might seem so: had I meant that I would have cut it out of the text. But 'shell-shock' is a state which can be arrived at in peace-time—this much medicine I *did* learn: symptoms which came to soldiers on the Somme can come to civilians working in an office block way above even the minor dangers of traffic. We breed terrors inside our-selves to match most of what we make of the world: and even the atom bomb—even that I have read some people consider to be planted in their stomachs. What I am trying to get the courage to write is how to *claim* courage for a man of thirty half-stoned on sleeping pills waking up in his own bathroom on the Saturday night of an August Bank Holiday when it is dark and he is instantly assaulted by terrors and yet, when all this is written, he is still a 'big strong man' lying on the floor safe from the outside world, bodily sound, of some intelligence, well enough off in any material sense—in what way at all can you be drawn to believe in his courage which you must believe in to make the rest of this story work? For we all must have some courage in some way—often: and most often of all those ways are ways which would embarrass us to discuss with more than one or two intimates and even with them we take care and refuge in the easier shallows of jokes and irony. Small perhaps daily acts which once we cringed at, fought against but had to do and now pretend we do not mind but only because we have forced our feelings into the emotional neutral of habit. Courage in crossing the road for some—is it too ridiculous to equate on the one hand the grand romantic courage of a gallant officer on a white horse galloping scarlet-tunicked galloping, galloping into the cannon's mouth—and a fragile dying old woman rising and dressing and taking a journey halfway across a county which pains her to the centre of her heart and makes her body tremble with such effort as must drive on its ruin, but will take this journey for an ideal of love and a notion of duty, and for that braves what are merely bumpy buses and empty shelters?

And I, too, claim courage for myself that night when I woke up bandaged in towels, stiff my skin, the feeling of it like leather on itself for I—what I there was—'I' was a rapids of streaming blood: all that was 'I' was blood, and the images in my mind were of old faded photographs, of family and friends, of faces half-known and scarcely noticed, of bomb sites and abandoned railway trucks, empty streets and broken windows, wastelands and falling houses; photographs in black and white through which the blood seeped, making them as brown as if they were being slowly burnt and then the reality the photographs copied would spring up as if in

138

its image's defence and there would *be,* would *exist,* mother, father, Lizzie, my daughter, Rod, all strangers, all, and the places of my time and my life until they too would be covered over with this blood; blood—yet it had no colour; it made things brown like a drained river bottom; brown like the oozing swamp we might have come out of: yet, and those glints and sharp points in my mind, those cuts which made me cry out, those razor slashes from a delinquent conscience—they glittered like minerals: but what there was of me—what I knew of me as I lay there—was nothing but movement and fear, nothing I saw as my own life.

When that life came it came as rats from the swamp, as snakes from the warm mud, as all the frightening and infected animals I'd seen in pictures and nightmares; and from that neat and carefully arranged bathroom, from imagined crevices and non-existent holes clambered a hungry, putrifying, plague-sored company of fear.

And this time there was no chance of help: no one to aim for on the other side of a street, no one to wait for, no crowd which would eventually deliver a point of outside interest. I tried to shout: I opened my mouth and did what I had always done in order to shout but no sound came or if it did I did not hear it. Then I began to shiver: and then, perhaps with relief, though more likely as an effort at healing—I began to shake, shake as if I'd been powerfully injected with a chemical I could not at all tolerate, shake at all my joints so that I was helpless to control it. But out of it, or in it, I found something of myself—an image of myself—I *saw* myself shaking on that floor at that time and it was in that way, through that mirror, that I stepped to some imitation of existence.

I rolled over and lost the towels: the side of the bath was so cold against my skin and clammed against it so firmly that I had a vision of the skin peeling away should I move. I held on to the side of the bath to stop myself shaking and tried to pull myself up. I kept slipping down onto my knees. Neither arms nor legs had sufficient strength for me to stand up. My teeth chattered: like a comic in a haunted house, my teeth 'chattered' and again an image—Lou Costello in a Haunted House in a Hollywood movie which had terrified me so much as a child that I'd slid under my cinema seat—that, too, helped me. And one thought, a single thought which came as slowly to my mind that I (who saw its approach and somehow simultaneously knew its message though not yet delivered)—I screamed inside myself as if urging on a racehorse whose victory would 'save my life': the thought which was a truth—that if I did not stand, if I did not fight here, now; then in some irrecoverable way I was finished: if not 'found dead on the bathroom floor' nor even 'found babbling and an idiot forever after' then at the very least numb both to my past personality which I had broken out of and broken up and to my future self which had yet to be hunted down and discovered.

I stood and still shaking I managed to put on my dressing-gown. I was almost exhausted, my strength almost gone: I needed help. Still without daring to put on a light I faced the bathroom door which itself faced the door of my flat and let myself 'go'—as it were—'fall' towards it.

I opened it and there was a shriek of affected fright; an unforgettable, it seems, mindless, unnecessary, stupid, vulgar, shrill, nervous, malign shriek which sliced into my mind and I heard myself moan. Two men 'leapt up': they had been sitting on the stairs, drinking: Geoffrey's party was under way—there were two other men leaning against the wall in the hall and from the front room came a discreet chattering hubbub, glasses clinking; they were well-behaved parties.

The man who had shrieked said 'Oh my Gawd!'

and put his hand to his mouth as if blocking a hiccup; then he bit his bottom lip, flicked a glance at his friend to register (what was obvious to all: all of them were looking at me now) astonishment and then repeated in the same affected genteel Cockney 'Oh my Gawd. You all right?' He giggled: but through nervousness only; he was concerned and I thankful for that.

Geoffrey came out of the front room and into the hall and, as soon as he saw me, he ran straight up the stairs. He looked very determined and did not excuse himself as he brushed past his guests. He took my arm, turned me back into my flat, put on the light and shut the door. 'Got any drink in the house then?' he asked gently and briskly.

I could not reply: I could say nothing: he put my arm around his shoulder and half dragged me into my front room where he switched on a light, a side light—he rejected the main one—and put me in a chair. Then he drew the curtains, put on another side light, glanced rapidly around the room and said, 'Now don't worry. You've had a turn—I can see that. I'll be one minute only: one minute.'

'Don't go. Please. Please. Please. Please. I—will—not — be — able — to — stay — together — please — please—please—please. Don't. Don't.'

He came back in with a large glass.

'Brandy. Now I want a big drink. Come on. Head up: mouth open. I'll lift it. There. Swallow—swallow—that's right. Now some more. Don't try to speak. Just let it go down you. Again—come on—don't give up—doesn't matter if it dribbles on your dressing-gown, they're *made* for stains, all right? Not even a smile. Swallow it. Swallow. You *are* in a state aren't you. And that eye of yours is giving out substance. Yes. Here. My hankie'll have to do for the moment. It was clean out tonight. There now. Now sit back. Hold the glass. No! You *must* hold it! You've got to pull yourself together and hold that glass. That's right. It's something to hold on to.'

The glass stuck in my palm like a cricket ball which had rocketed there so hard that it had sealed itself to the skin: the chunky cut-glass felt just as solid and definite.

Geoffrey sat down on my settee-bed and lay back, drawing up his legs. He was wearing brown and beige: a beige shirt, tight beige trousers and beige socks: brown leather boots and a brown silk scarf and a massive brown belt, thick and wide, decorated with imitation silver bullets, nine on each side of the buckle. I imagined one of them snug in the cold, open labyrinth of my brain. I stared at him: he was not at all disconcerted.

'Have another sip,' he said, 'it'll take effect soon. There's about a quarter of a bottle in that glass! Go on—drink up.'

I did as he said.

'I knew you were in a bad way this morning,' he said, and again spoke so gently and soothingly that I felt my shoulders weaken, a wave of self-pity break inside me threatening tears. 'I knew it wasn't just your eye. You looked so tensed up—"uptight" they'd say—I hate all that hippie slang, don't you? It's so meaningless. Don't bother to answer; you just sit nice and quiet and try to relax. Let that brandy get to work, that's the only thing can do you any benefit tonight.

'You ought to get out more—you won't mind me saying so, will you? But I've noticed—you're a very private sort of person and very sort of on your own, isolated, you know? It gets you down, that sort of thing. I tried to kill myself twice you know—yes; twice. You looked like I felt when I saw you on those stairs. It was Harold who pulled me out of it—not by anything he did, just by what *is*, you understand; he's no boy wonder but you couldn't meet a kinder person. I think that very emotional people like us—we need somebody, you know, down-

142

beat, calm, a bit more ordinary, to keep us all from jumping off the Post Office Tower. And nothing could be more ordinary than being an accountant, I tell you: I don't know how he sticks it. When he comes home and tells me what he's been doing—and all the fiddles that people want to get up to! Mind you, Harold's incorruptible, I'll say that much.

'Better now? Another drink? Go on. And don't worry that you're keeping me. I told Harold you'd had a turn: he understood. We hardly *need* to talk to each other about important things—that's what's so marvellous about it.

'Can I look round? You *do* have a lot of lovely things here: good *taste*. I like those paintings: they'll be nineteenth-century copies, won't they? Not very *good* but very decorative: nice. And that grey chair you're in is *really* nice: Victorian isn't it? No mirrors, I see; we have mirrors everywhere. I'm terrible for looking at myself: it used to bother me, you know, now I just accept it; the funny thing is I don't do it as much. Something psychological about that, I'm sure.

'You must be very clever to read all those books and I'm sure you have. You're not the sort of person to use *books* to impress anybody. They're part of what you do, aren't they—books?

'Better?

'Oh, what a beautiful thing! I *love* the colours in Roman glass. Oh, it's beautiful. It's a phial, isn't it, for tears, I've seen one before. They put them up to their eyes like this and then cried a bit and then corked it up; it's a funny idea for us to appreciate but there's something sort of *moving* about it even if you don't understand.

'It was a lovely girl came to see you today, if you don't mind my remarking on it. Really. I'm sorry I grabbed you when you came back in from old Smell—that's what *I* call him—but he makes me so mad. He's so *rude*. Rude people are just not worth it: he's *awful* to Veronica: that's his wife, do you know her? Well we often have a chat when she's in the garden and I'm in the kitchen. I just open the window and we chatter away. He's so *rude* to her.

'Better now?'

He stayed for almost half an hour and talked without any interruption from myself who swung between extreme fragility and leaden—(how apt clichés become when you have known the situation)—leaden tiredness. He stayed until he could guess with some certainty that I had 'settled down'. Then, with many protestations as to his availability should I need further help, he took the glass and left me.

I had not said a word: had I been able to speak I would have said 'thank you' and 'don't leave me' and alternated so between gratitude and timidity.

I knew I was in no condition to stay on my own: the sounds from his party below, the accelerated roar of the cars below dive-bombing on the black and unpoliced Heath, the heat of the day which was now intensifying; I needed company. I have not spent much time trying to describe the heat to you: it seemed to me that my form of broken narrative would not lend itself to such reiteration which of course added to the charge of the day but in this story would too soon have become too obvious a signpost. But now it is important to know that the city heat choked the pores, rubbed itself coarsely in my throat and somehow pressed on the street, battened on it, gave it less and less breath and less and less ease. And my eye was flickering badly: I had been carrying my sunglasses since putting on my dressing-gown: I replaced them now.

Geoffrey *had* given me help and I capitalized on it right away. With what appeared to me at the time to be remarkable speed but was most probably sluggish and feeble, I dressed: I put on my best black suit, a white

144

shirt and a flowered tie which I took off, leaving my shirt open at the neck. I went into the bathroom—bathed my eye and sloshed cold water on my face: the sleeping tablets and the brandy sucked at my mind. I would have liked to go with the calling pressure but did not trust it, for suppose it took me into sleep only to let me wake up at three o'clock in the morning? What would I do then? I would not have the courage to call for help at 3 a.m. Too dramatic: rules are stronger than instinct. Right, left and right again. I needed to be really tired and certain for sleep; no chances taken.

Then I phoned Eileen: a girl answered with a voice exactly like hers.

'Eileen?'

'No.'

'Is that Eileen?'

'Eileen's out. Who's that?'

'When will she be back? It's urgent.' It was. It was the most urgent call I'd made or could think of making. Eileen would be interested, she would understand and my fears would melt away.

'Who *is* it?'

'A friend of hers. . . .' I did not want to give my name to this stranger with such an exasperated tone, such an assumed right to know who I was.

'Well I'm afraid I can't help you.'

'My name's Ted Johnson. She was—she's a friend of mine.'

'Who?'

'TED. JOHNSON.'

'*Ted.* Oh. I thought she was with you. She said she was going out to see you. That was hours ago. I thought she *was* with you.' She sounded very suspicious.

'I see. Thank you.'

'I say, have you any idea where she might be? I mean, she *ought* to be with *you*.'

145

'No. . . . Sorry.' I put the phone down as she drew breath for another question.

I went to the door of my flat and opened it, gently. No one was on the stairs; only two people were in the hall. I hurried down the stairs, along the hall, outside, and up towards the High Street.

The heat and noise and possibilities of London met me and blew into me as they might have played on an instrument: I felt I was theirs. I had been myself in coming out. Now I had delivered myself into the hands of all that might be enemies to do their worst; to get it over with; to be defeated or to win.

*   *   *   *

I try to keep in the story all that can apply to as many people as possible; I am always conscious of the tints which have been added to me by an extended and expensive education and part of my trouble that day was to do with some part of me rejecting that education violently. If you want to see such a small thing as my finding myself—in the extreme situation—to be dressed in exactly the same way as the 'tough' who was on the other side of the street when I arrived at the top of it, obviously waiting for either Wendy's return or my exit —if you want you can see that as an indication, small but nevertheless a sign of a wish to return to what I might have been had I not been interfered with by the state and altered by my surrender to pressures I did not really appreciate. But then, I had welcomed the interference and taken it to be an embrace: hence, perhaps, the sunglasses I still wore and which, at night, could only look affected no matter that my eye was streaming steadily.

Again and here most anti-dramatically, I jib before the next fence of the story. Nevertheless, I began to write fiction and undertake the difficulties and the work this

146

involved for many subsidiary reasons and one of them was most certainly to tell people what it was like, to show them my record and in that way to help them if possible. I believe that where possible fiction like all imaginative writing should be helpful; the very best is beautiful *and* truthful and instances of those aspects of life are all the help we need. Even this (and I would be selling out on myself if I tried to shuffle out of it) can be of use: for I believe that most of you have tried to escape from what you have been made, what you believe has been MADE of you when your will was unformed or uncertain or beguiled. And it may be that, like the man in this story, your attempt can be made to appear of little importance and negligible interest. Oh! they would say, all he wants is to leave home, all she's after is getting out of the village, all they want to do is be different, grow their hair too long, wear their skirts too short; whatever. Anything can be dismissed by those not involved: even holocausts are of small concern to those utterly unconnected—how many Chinese were shaken by the First World War?—yet to those involved. . . .

So I say this. I stood on the corner of that street looking with no prospect of defence at the man across from me who was certainly my enemy and hesitated only because he was also waiting for Wendy. I felt lost; I had abandoned hope in myself—submitted to the circumstances, and though I could name neither the source nor the form of it, nor tell you the extent nor the weight of it, I knew myself to be in danger.

The heat seemed to crackle about in the fumey air of the High Street, restlessly urging it on to greater agitation. And the cars streaming up from London and into Hampstead or through it, for the suburban reaches up the northern highways. The sounds of the cars that night reached that point of affliction which the aeroplanes had so soon arrived at when I'd lived in the south-west on a route to Heathrow Airport: then my mind, at times, had been like the strings on the bow of a violin and the ceaseless passages of the brake-screaming planes like fierce attacks of a bow upon it—violent slashings of catgut, aimed at inflicting pain and harm on their object. Of a different quality but with just as distressing an effect were those Saturday-night cars.

My mind by then was assuming many shapes of fear; and to sound it was like a valley of echo chambers. I imagined I heard the fair from the Heath, the noise of London coming up through the deep orange sky which hung above it like a glow over a destroyed city, and shouts in the streets were like war-cries.

What ought to have mitigated against this, softened it, humanized it and made it seem silly, was the casual, elegant, leisured flow of young people walking up the hill towards the Hampstead pubs. There was only easy movement and a corporate sense of style. I had no ease of body—had even to order it to move at all—and my style was that of the man who looked as I might have looked had I left school at fifteen and stayed in my town: I was not part of the elegance drifting past, nor of the hardness standing undecided.

I went across to him. His hands were in his trouser pockets; he did not take them out. I wanted to say:

'Look. *You* think I'm Wendy's boyfriend. I'm not. She's out. If you were here you must have seen her go out. I don't know where she's gone and I don't know when she'll come back. It's absurd for you to "tail" me like this. There's nothing in it for you and you make me jumpy. I'm not well and you're making me worse. Forget Wendy. She wants nothing to do with you. Forget her and me and all of this and go away.'

I said nothing.

He interpreted my silence as a challenge; a 'weighing up'. He rocked slightly on his heels and balanced himself, more ready to fight. I wanted to speak and I tried to speak but my heart was racing, thundering against my rib cage, almost drilling it so fast was it moving and my throat was as sore as if a length of rough hemp had been dragged up and down it since morning.

I turned and left him.

*   *   *   *

To my left down the hill was London and there the treasure which was the prize of my education and wage and ambition—theatres, galleries, concerts, opera, and, even at this time of night, films, jazz, good pop and clubs —'culture': what I'd been primed for; my powder. I had to believe in that; I had nothing else, nothing else at all and I do not talk here of subscriptions—I pay my occasional dues to charity and in a modest way heave on the barge of reform when the rope passes through my hands—I talk here of what the conscious part of a lifetime had aimed for. Down there was the Culture which I'd worked to understand, to enter, to deal with: now I needed help *it* should help me.

I had not the strength to go down into London, but I'd seen a film advertised, *Hiroshima Mon Amour*, at the Everyman Cinema just up the street in the centre of Hamstead. Here, as often when people are in deadliest earnest, you can savour another example of the ridiculous. Though let me be honest—it was not ridiculous to me, however ridiculous I appear to you. I knew I'd seen that film, and it demonstrated much of what modern 'culture' could offer. It was set in Hiroshima and some of it took place in the museum which housed 'relics' from the city after the dropping of the Atom Bomb (nothing more cultured than the atom; nothing more modern than The Bomb). It was to do with memory and desire, to do with the sort of life you ought to lead and the life you'd got or wanted. It was written by a French writer whose novels were strange and, I thought, strained, but compelling, often unnerving—a real writer, and directed by a distinguished French director. In every way it was the 'culture' of our time—essentially of *my* time—as the cinema is for my generation 'our' art form.

There was always a late show on Saturdays and I walked up there; once more along the High Street, blotchy with lights and still the movement up the hill. No need to say that the simple walk there clawed at my mind. Past me went the youth, dreamy, peaceful. I could have wept from bitter envy and frustration. All was calm, all was bright.

Outside the cinema I hesitated. The queue had gone in. I pretended to myself that I did not mind missing the beginning and so I looked at the photographs outside. But really I feared to be enmeshed in a regimented crowd as much as I had feared to be uncontrollably alone. There is no health in us.

Looking at the photographs was enough. Charged with need, my mind recalled the film and I remembered it clearly. There was a Japanese man and a French woman talking to him. She was talking most of the time, urgently, rapidly, tensely; pouring herself into the vat of his love; love that was calling on her to give him her deepest secret. I knew that love. I had told Lizzie of the time my father had slashed at my mother with a knife, gashing her arm and then, in terror at his act, gone into the allotment and slept in the shed, refusing to come back into the house for three days: that and other times of shame; dearest, deepest secrets all seem buried in shame. She was offering him this, and then you saw what she was talking about. Another photograph. A young girl in Occupied France having an affair with a German, an enemy soldier—lyrically in love with him. In a small town like my own.

She had talked on and on. My body was rigid, my feet tense against the pavement as if pushing myself away from it: still my heart beat loudly and even in that deserted sideway I was afraid the sound might be heard.

Then you saw her lover, the German, shot, dead, and she lying beside him, crying. At the thought of it tears came to my own eyes and ran down my face.

They shaved her head. The other women of the town shaved her head to punish her for loving their enemy; and she was locked in a cellar. There was a photograph of that: light from barred windows. I began to fear that I might shout out. To be locked below the street, to be locked alone, alone in a dark cellar, head shaved and in shame. The whole town which had known you however odd you might have been, however 'quiet'; the small town which you had loved and in which you had found a love—for that to turn so viciously against you that you were locked out of it and had no place in it, could never, never get back in it but must have her head shaved and be locked away in a special room, becoming an 'object' of especial interest. The child kicked in my throat.

I began to sob. The child swam up and I could see it in my throat, suffocating.

I went up the cul de sac a little way, leaned against the wall and cried. There was nothing more I could do. There was nothing she could do. She had had a love and lost it; I too. That was all. There are a million greater tragedies and a million greater losses each day the planet turns. But I had remembered her and seen her in the cellar and I knew what she felt and I cried aloud until I was tired and calmer.

I had been facing the wall. Tentatively I turned around. I had been unregarded.

There was nowhere for me to go but Rod's party. I

151

walked slowly, dabbing at my eye with my handkerchief, hoping that sweat from the heat would somehow ease off the tracks of the tears.

Alone in that cellar: poor woman: for love.

8

Rod had taken care to get his party right, I thought; and even my late invitation was somehow part of the preparation—a casual flourish which merely exercised his confidence. I had been welcomed and directed to the drinks' table, told to help myself with 'booze and a bite', and left alone. I was now clear-headed and heavily tired: I'd scarcely eaten anything all day and was more than content to assemble a plateful of food, take a long whisky, find a comfortable chair, feed myself and look about.

I am weary at the prospect of describing this party in detail and yet, as near the beginning when I insisted on rattling off a quick guide to Hampstead, so here; there are reasons for this. Perhaps it might be possible to relate them: for as Hampstead represented what I hoped to meet in London, so Rod and his party represented what I then wanted to be in London. That's rather glib and it sells me short, but there's enough in it for it to be a useful summary. Of course I would never have admitted, then, that I envied the people at Rod's and wanted to be like them and in some ways I did not: but in a sufficient number of ways I did—sufficient enough for the admission to be useful.

I am weary not because of the event then but because of events now. Fiction writers must lock themselves in the cellars of their own making and never even want to come out. I must feed my mother. She eats little: she is patient and cheerful. I read to her—I'm reading *Pride and Prejudice* to her at the moment and we're often

153

absorbed, the two of us, in this third world, happy to be bound together there. At times we are happier than we have ever been. All that I might have held against her; all that I hated her for, and blamed us together for, is suspended: we live in a hushed and timeless present. So peaceful is it that my father comes in now without more than a ripple and is bemused by the tranquillity of it all and his surprise makes us all self-conscious; we wonder why it could not be like this 'before'.

The stories which best capture this relationship between the active present and fiction are those very short anecdotes of Chekhov. He wrote each one in a few hours and you can feel the day in them: the man has been seen in the street with snow on the back of his coat, the young woman has pleaded with Dr Chekhov across a sick relative, the egotist has developed a mournful monologue on his hospital bed. Chekhov's day as a doctor—his busy day—is as much in the stories, 'informs' them as strongly as any notion of 'a story', and is as potent as the anecdote itself.

This is to switch from whales to minnows—but I wish I had some way of 'informing' this story with her death. And yet—as soon as I'd written that, I felt as if I'd been grossly indiscreet. The implication is, of course, that her dying somehow serves my purpose and the conclusion which that points to is that I am somehow capitalizing on it. In short, benefit where I should be bereft if my feelings are what I say they are. I look up and see that beautifully decorated room of Rod's full of successful people—generally good-looking, some beautiful, all well-dressed, some 'exquisite'—and then look out at the terraced houses across the street, bars against my window panes, images of my own fixed place which I cannot leave now at my own will, and remember half an hour ago when she fell asleep as I read to her

154

and I put her arms under the blankets, smoothed her hair and left her peacefully sleeping.

Much earlier, I said something to the effect that I was content for this limited time to play the son she cast me as. Yet in the playing the character has grown much like my own. I consider it most fortunate that I should be so available for her and so able to do everything for her when she needs it most. She is in pain but I am sure the pleasure she has in our attendance on each other makes that pain endurable: she might even, I think, welcome the pain or at least be more than willing to trade it for these serene scenes, this filial piety, her own undeniably noble manner, the perfect sunset which forgets the storm of the day.

So that I might in some way escape from this conjunction it will be in Rod's own tones, perhaps, if I manage to mimic him well, in something of the colour of his thoughts—certainly in line with his general ideas —that I will introduce this party. It makes sense. I was sitting outside it all: next to me some people were talking earnestly about Harold Wilson and John Lindsay as if they were personal friends: near enough for alternative eavesdropping were a trio devoted to films, 'playing' together beautifully, each entering on exactly the right note at precisely the right time and building up a little buzz of appreciative harmony. I will, perhaps, come back to them—but I am eating pygmy sausages and sandwiches the size of a ten-bob bit, sipping whisky and counting in fractions, pleased that my eye is momentarily quiet again but even more pleased to be wearing dark glasses as somehow it provides me with the 'touch' I need (so badly), makes me grata here; someone: not like the poor relation I had been with other of Rod's charity tickets to his entertainments. And finally, you see, I am in no mood to be fair to him. Better try to pretend to be him: mind you, it will not be easy because he has so far set his books in various backwaters of that backwater Cumberland part of that backwater the North West of England. People are impressed by this; taking the contrast between his fashionable London Life and his unfashionable novels to be proof of integrity: whereas, of course, it's nearer schizophrenia and *much* more like sentimentality.

His party: while I sit and wait; there and here.

*   *   *   *

'Ted looked awful. At first I thought he was pissed and I was glad. He ought to get pissed more often—sluice the starch out of him. He wore dark glasses and no tie which was unexpected and it made him look rather—dashing?—acceptable certainly which was a relief. I was fed up with his sleeveless pullovers and bulk-bought suits—we all know about devotion and self-sacrifice. When I saw he'd been crying I took him into the corner and sat him on some eats and scotch; it was a low lights and low interest area—the records and the dancing space were at the other end, the more private clusters had found their niches on stairs or in other rooms. What he needed was to be left alone and I did that.

'This house is in a smart street: one of the smartest in the centre of the town. If you are part of the 'puritan' (so-called: rather a large claim for the current level of your activity) segment of this society then prepare to have your squeamishness fully aroused. In 1956 these cottages were offered to their working-class tenants for £800 but with so much small print that the tenants understandably refused and cleared out: alternative accommodation was not too difficult to find then. Whereupon, forewarned by chance, half the houses in the street were bought up by a single developer who developed and sold them for £7,000 each—four bedrooms, two reception, one kitchen, one bath, small garden and a shower. In 1966 I bought mine for £13,500: I put

£2,500 into it. I could sell it for £23,000. A short history of the expanding mid-century affluence of middle-class England is thus presented you in four progressively shorter sentences.

'My next move ought to be to Chelsea where many of my acquaintances, and most of those in my sort of business and on my income level, live. But I might leap-frog that stage and arrive in Knightsbridge or Belgravia in one. Depends partly on my accountant, partly on my stamina and partly, dear reader, on my public.

'Ah yes! More squirming called for. I have a public and I pay attention to it. My television programmes hope to capture its interest and hold it. I don't serve up pap but neither do I preach. Remember that one of the working-class heroes is the successful bookie with a Jaguar, a swimming pool, and a blonde on either arm, and you will understand as much about the majority in England as from all *The Road to Wigan Pier*.

' "Knowing" the public means "knowing" about reactions: for example, I have little doubt that most of you who would have the time, education, interest and money to read such a book as this will be irritated by almost everything I have written since my "entrance". You will feel ruffled by what you will consider to be not only an objectionable attitude but a false, embarrassed and defensive pose.

'Correct.

'After that first paragraph (which is why I said you would be irritated by "almost" everything: my first paragraph was acceptable because of its concern for others), I *did* begin in a defensive way and then continued for the hell of it; and will go on for much the same reason. It is refreshing to be away from my own concerns— from feeding the silent majority through the tube, so carefully cooking the mix; to preparing a novel for its safe passage past the scrutiny of searching scores—I come here to enjoy myself and stretch a bit as people came to my party. And of course another important explanation of my attitude is that I resent the general and lazy contemporary expectation that a smart party in a smart house full of smartly-dressed people will inevitably be phoney, boring, affected, "worthless" and comical. As that is the common "in" cant—I will be at pains to rebuff it: onward.

"For it is just another face of "The rich are so un-happy" myth. The rich, it has been discovered since Freud replaced Kipling on the Headmaster's bookshelf—the rich are no more unhappy than the poor: as it is now discovered they are no more evil—remember the Needle's Eye?—"It is easier for a camel"—and so on than for a rich man to enter the Kingdom of God? What a comfort *that* was to the poor! And before that, the rich had to be kings and warriors for they alone were "pure" enough to be sacrificed to the gods. Poor old them! Always we've found something to pin on them: no longer. I tell you, I hope I'm on my way to being rich and I'm just exactly as screwed up as I always was only I've more loot and so the chance to stymie myself in style. Poor little rich boy? Bollocks! You have fooled yourselves and been fooled for long enough—"hurry, hurry, hurry", ladies and gentlemen, brush off the anti-money taboos which the powerful and the clever have caused to fall on you like a curse which they renew from generation to generation; "hurry, hurry, hurry": money can bypass ideals as completely as a new high-way can cut off a sleepy little village—think of the heartache some people have endured to help feed the hungry in India and see now what the (dirty?) money from a great American foundation has produced with its ten-crop-a-year-strain of rice—or do you believe in the value of suffering? Do you believe it is *better* to be unhappy because there is (somehow) "worth" in it— in which case you are against, among others, Aristotle and Tolstoy, both of whom declare that happiness is man's greatest end and, more important, you are against common sense—"hurry, hurry hurry" (see how I fit in with the fair which was going on at the same time as my party? I had been there earlier in the evening with half a dozen others and "hurry, hurry, hurry" whirled around in my mind that night and would not go)—reject the philosophies of failure which is Tory philosophy and the values of a besieged life, which are Liberal values, and the ideals of a perfect life which are for perfect men but not for thee and me fair friend (what a relief to write a long sentence! In my novels they are of moderate length—occasionally shorter to break a rhythm, but moderate sentences: on television they are so short that Hemingway appears effusive by comparison)—and know that your enemy's enemy is your friend, know that sufficient unto the day, and know all the rest of the glorious fragments timidly hinting at the splendour of happiness—*open* the coffers, *shake* the rafters, *take* the plunge, *seize* the day, *make* the gesture and watch the ice caps of the world jump off with delight!

'The people who came to my party were no mugs.

'I will stress here that my general remarks should in no way lead you to believe that either myself or the people I know are heartless. Many of them are energetically involved in work which would command your sympathy and even your applause. They are not the foot sloggers it is true: they much admire the foot sloggers and here I can hardly say that Ted is someone I *much* admire. He works too hard for too little, trying to pick up the leavings of the university system at that technical college of his: if he could get himself straightened out a little he could easily get a more enjoyable job. I believe he sticks it out of a sense of duty: just as he will patiently canvass door-to-door for the Labour Party on rainy nights for local elections, just as he once joined in dismal demonstrations and walked miles from borough to borough bearing placards protesting against evictions or empty houses or whatever: he will not have told you about this himself and this comes, I'm sure, not only from reticence but also from a certain embarrassment. For he never became a "demonstrator", never one of the automatic protest effort (note my neat initials: patented): he is too interesting to be content with the boringness of black and white: English society is not black and white—this infuriates romantics but is the relish of realists. Yet—when all is said—was Ted's effort for the Labour Party either more courageous or more effective than mine? I spoke for our Labour candidates on several platforms and at several large dinners; not door to door, nor heart to heart, but head to head: *and* there was risk. It doesn't do to be too closely identified with one party when you're on television. You may have noted the emasculation of your TV presenters: eunuchs are often kings in that strange country. It's the law of the land. My "image" of course, as you know, goes against all that.

'Let me situate the party.

'My home is professionally decorated and the furniture came either from a good store or a reliable antique shop. I have a large collection of records, particularly early jazz, "pop" and eighteenth-century chamber music; and some decent contemporary paintings. I have, or rather there is, an Irish housekeeper—Mary it is she's called an' all after the Virgin Herself which she is too without question, never a question—and between her and the woman I live with at the moment, Jane, a freelance journalist, rich family and extremely "refined" taste—the place is kept together and so am I.

'The "guests": would that I had an ornate list to photostat and print on this page for you to study at length but alas it was a matter of an hour on the

160

telephone the evening before to get a few people together on Jane's insistence because it was my birthday. Isn't that nice! Insofar as I have a circle of friends those present would be segment of the circle. Jane has intimate friends; girls she was at school with and so on: she stepped into a silk-lined purse of a set up when *she* came to London (your working classes have only dreams and disappointments compared with the subtly graded ambitions and jealousies, the wish and the envy of those of us born at some stepping point along that broad and easy—sic—way of the middle classes). I invited a few of the people who work with me: there were others before them and will be others after them—we are good working friends. The only constant names in my book are the established, the entrepreneur and the essential —doctor, solicitor, accountant, broker, agent, dentist and publisher.

'Most of those there that night had been born, like myself, with some money behind them. Most with more than me. "To him that hath shall be given." It's in the bible, missis, God's truth.

'Here I hesitate. Why *should* I begin to particularize about these people? As my guests they enjoy my protection. (Oh—we have time for all this with money in the bank, Oh yes, indeed we do; "honour", "manners", "taste"—you name it, we display it). They are all, all of them, people who are on the way to the top which means that they have luck or talent or courage (none of which any sane person could ever despise), or all three. Many of them look as good as they think: some much better. Few would find it difficult to make £4,000 a year (except Ted, of course, and one or two others); most make more, some quite a bit more than that. And in case you imagine I am talking about a tiny minority—it is bigger than you imagine and many are rushing to join. They're honest people: they pay all their taxes—which are extremely heavy; they tend to have to pay high rates, high prices for their houses, their food, the garaging of their cars, and so on. Few are in "regular" jobs. I would say that Ted was about the sole guest there with expectation of a pension—except for a producer from the BBC and even he's freelance now, I believe, and so out on his own. Money has to go into insurances and private pension schemes. Believe me, Oh ye in Cumberland, eighty quid a week does not in *fact* mean that you live much better in terms of essentials than say twenty or thirty: I know many people in Cumberland on about thirty/forty pounds a week much better off materially than people in London on two or three times as much. Which is not to say that it isn't nice to get two or three times as much.

'As you see I'm a tory who votes Labour. A "Left Conservative" as Norman Mailer so charmingly and conveniently puts it: meaning, as I do, I suppose, that we can lash out in all directions because of course we are privileged, we are part of the officer corps in this hierarchic country and the officer class does pretty well. We are *not* as obnoxious as the out-and-out upper-class hegemonists who through the City, the big corporations and the many departments of state and public service open to a closed circle, still control—that is the word—large areas of the lives of the majority: we are officers, mostly, who got our promotion in the field and think very highly of our "men". We are not unlike those tortured people in the poems and books on the First World War—those sensitive young blades who suddenly realized that *their* word could make flesh—die. We *care*. But of course, in any general context, in any dialectical analysis, even to a feeble revolutionary—one of those underfed, Afro-haired boyos who from time to carefully scheduled time feature in my studio programme—we are part of *them*, the bosses, and should be pulled down.

'But. This is England—1970. We are *not* in a revolutionary situation and everyone at my party knows it. The shop stewards may be challenging the Unions and the Unions may shout and shout louder but society in this country is not threatened with revolution. It could be reformed: or it could submit to the cultivated and convenient sense of apathy, established ways, small businesses and orderly queues. I need not say that everyone at my party wanted reform. You may laugh: some of them were risking a little who had a lot to lose.

'We are not the masters.

'You will want to know how much this small impromptu party cost me. About £100: it was not on expenses. Dress?—the usual present jumble display—but of course it was Biba's rather than the local boutique and sometimes a glossy whizz-kid rather than Biba's. And the subjects of conversation? Ah!

'One man was talking about Lester Piggott and challenging his foe to think of an artist as dedicated to his art as Piggott is to riding race-horses. The foe said Michelangelo. The man asked for a contemporary saying the past was another country (a "hidden" quotation from L. P. Hartley: this man is a politician in his early thirties, exceptionally talented, already a noted and impressive M.P.—and this is one of his twelve favourite quotations: they are the opening words of the novel *The Go-Between*: "The past is a foreign country; they do things differently there.") The foe was stumped. Did this, then, the politician said, mean that art could not occupy a man's life as completely and exclusively as horse-racing? Very likely, said the foe, but then one had to consider the quality of the activity—a boring old question but was even riding the Derby winner "better" than writing an excellent poem? Who was to judge and by whose standards and what did you mean by "better"? returned the politician, a clear winner at this stage. And, interpolated a drunken gloomy man in a green velvet jacket, a playwright whose reputation outshone

163

his success to the disgust of his vanity though the succour of his pride—and, he said, "It is a solemn and serious question; who is to judge whether it is 'better' for a writer to get pissed or read Proust? If Lester Piggott gets pissed he will be unsteady in the saddle the next day: the drunkenness of a writer might release him from a nag he has been saddled with too long. . . ."

'There was an intricate analysis of the American Left, more of a seminar than a discussion—conducted by a black American actor who was over here to star in a television play. . . . There was a most desultory dispute about pornography—desultory because only one of the three participants was interested and the more she exclaimed that she wanted "more of it" the less the others appeared capable of anything at all. . . . One or two minor incidents—natural in a crowded room. . . . People chatted about other people: most people did that. It was a chatty party: most of those people used these sort of parties to find out what past friends or future acquaintances were up to. . . . Alright. Scandals were retailed, bust marriages were the most common property and yet, though interest was taken and often amusement derived from the descriptions, these people were themselves sufficiently scarred to be decent. We were not a "set" who prided ourselves either on our monogamy or on our licence: we were not, really, a "set". Pop music the whole time. A few couples danced.

'Where did we work? Journalism, television, publishing, films, advertising, acting, universities, the law, the more light-hearted businesses, the more interesting civil service departments: LONDON. The great majority were "loners": freelance is the professional term.

'Finally. Who are they? No names, no pack drill.'

*   *   *   *

164

How do I pick up from there? The validity, to me, of putting the description of the party into Rod's 'mouth' has been unbalanced by 'his' garrulousness. I am only in some measure playing games: I put myself in the position to put his point of view and he had a great deal to say, much more than I have written down but a bite is a feast—from him. (I find it difficult, now, not to imitate him.) And I thought it important to demonstrate by that single example how out of key my feeling of disintegration was—and how irrelevant. I did feel irrelevant. And somehow the fact that my appearance enabled me to fit in made me even more irrelevant: for usually at Rod's parties I'm so badly dressed and so awkward that he needs to whisper my worthy credentials to a generous acquaintance of his or throw me in neck and crop with the never failing (I assure you: he had not forgotten) 'Tell us what Tutenkhamen did to Nefertiti.' And then I would stand and spout: like a broken gutter.

This time I merged: I sat quietly and took another whisky and discovered some of the minor powers of silence and withdrawal, for one or two women would, I think, have liked to chat but the self-absorption of my attitude—become more dense when even lightly threatened—put them off.

I tried to work out how I would get through the night on my own. There were two alternatives: to get 'dead' drunk, or to go into London to some of the all-night spots—I'd been to plenty of those in the fruitless 'testing' days: they were not very comfortable or they were far too expensive. I would get drunk.

Having made the decision I decided to move: some memory of politeness pushed its way through the débris of my mind and I heard my mother say, 'You ought to talk to people, Edward: it's not nice, just sitting there on your own like that: it makes others uncomfortable and isn't at all considerate to Roderick.'

I stood up and walked across the room and then, realizing my mistake, turned back. My seat had been taken by a tall girl who was already curled up in it affecting sleep: her shoes dropped off her feet, slowly, as if gently tugged off by invisible fingers. A man and a woman were talking near me and I half turned to be 'part' of them; but did not suck at their acknowledgement, wishing not to be involved. They understood such a position—perhaps the hook-on/hook-off craft is as recognizable to experienced party-goers as non-possessive territorial manoeuvres to other animals. It took me some time to master the fear I had, the uncertainty which came from having no base. I noticed little about the man except that he had a Welsh accent rather too broad for the apparent narrowness and speciality of his 'field' which he kept defining by saying what was 'outside' it. The woman was dressed in a deep purple trouser suit of light velvet; her face was most carefully made up. She spoke urgently and it was through her that I was again drawn *out* of myself; as I had been at the Fair. She needed to *know*—as soon as I paid attention I was filled with her fear. The man looked more and more uncomfortable and began flicking his eyes towards me—needing me to come in now, needing help. I'd been there long enough to have to earn my keep.

They were arguing and the room was interested. There was that quietening of volume among others, the sense that the evening was coming to its first climax, the satisfied sigh of expectation, the nervousness of those who guessed or who knew and the curiosity of those who were unaware, a time when the 'party' became indeed a single part, a body corporate, a thing which prowled around and moved and scented as one, with fifty eyes and hands and many brains—all 'homing' on that part of themselves which had overplayed, overacted; in some way was threatening to detach itself from the gentle protoplasm.

She was an American actress, intense and a little flurried. She spoke loudly:

'Of course the bloody thing's a fairy-tale. I mean, it's so old *fashioned* even to talk about it. To get it wrong as well is antediluvian. I mean, I can't even bring myself to contradict you. You needn't wave your hands like that—I mean, there's simply no sense in even discussing it in those terms.'

'Well then,' he was as over-gentle as she was over-forceful, 'Let's define our terms or rather let's discover them.'

'But, don't you see?' She was getting desperate: 'It isn't WORTH it! It just IS NOT WORTH discussing. Not in those terms.'

'Well then. That's—that's fine then. Let's forget it.'

'Oh, it's not that easy. Not once you've started. I mean it is THE most interesting AREA, and you can't just bring it up and then drop it as soon as we're getting down to it. Oh no. Oh no. Not that one.'

'Fine. So. Where should we begin?'

'Oh no. YOUR pitch. This is *your* pitch. That's right. I'm an American, I say pitch. Play. I'll say "play". Your play. Pitch is passée. Play. Your play.' She drank some more.

'Well,' said the Welshman, having observed the silence and lost some of the sympathy awaiting him by playing to it for too long, 'Well, let's state the problem in simple terms.'

'*Whose* problem? *Your* problem? *My* problem? *Whose* problem? *I* haven't got a problem. To me there is no problem. That's the POINT. And what's SO SIMPLE about THAT?'

'Really, this is—look, I'm sorry. I can't go on.'

'EXACTLY! HUH!'

There was silence: and as Rod moved forward and her boy friend moved forward the gentle Welshman said, politely but firmly:

167

'You're stoned.'

'You *bastard!*'

Rod and her boy friend arrived. The Welshman smiled shrugged and turned away. Conversation started up. The girl, abandoned to her two saviours, dropped her glass with a gesture meant to be a throw though whether she was moved by anger at the Welshman's insult or petulance at the sudden and general lack of interest it would be difficult to say. The glass broke and her whisky swam over an expensive-looking carpet.

'Oh, I'm sorry Rod. Rod, where's your . . . ? No, I'll be too late. I'll wipe it myself now.' She got on her knees scrubbing away with the tunic of her velvet suit and murmuring: 'Oh your beautiful carpet; your beautiful beautiful carpet.'

Rod and her friend smiled at each other with genuine amusement and in mutual appreciation. The man was American, and an actor, I later discovered.

'Come on Peg. Off your knees, gal. That way won't get you to hebben no sir.'

And the hush which had been at the centre of the politely renewed chat, the tense and nosy hush which had held its breath in hope of drama, laughed gently, realizing it was all over. Peg was got to her feet, taken out for a breath of 'London air' and brought back happy, smiling and apparently sober.

I relaxed, too, and used the freedom to pour myself some more whisky—a very strong one this time, three parts whisky one part water—in a long tumbler. Then I waited for the black actor to come back. I would stand beside him. He would talk, he would make the time pass, he would force attention, he would be my talisman. I could read no book; but I tried—hunched over it in a corner, waiting for him—I tried, and saw Rod looking at me and shrugged, trying to pretend or to convey that this was a mere digression in my evening, that a strong association had led me to look up a fact just to settle a doubt in my mind—and doing it was proof of ease, real casualness, spontaneity, all that our lot were supposed to be 'at', wasn't it? Rod understood. He left me alone. The print broke upon the page: it was horrible: it was like looking inside my own head. I almost passed out but closed my eyes tight, squeezing the bad left eye so that it hurt, using the hurt to keep me from passing out, keeping the book open to pretend I was still reading. There was a hard little lump on my eye now, a nasty hard little lump that hurt quite usefully when I squeezed it. I was grateful for that.

When he came back I stood near him: out of his eye-line but near him. Slightly behind him like Peg on the other side. Like Peg I said nothing. He spoke about the socialists and students in America: he spoke as if he were giving evidence at a vital hearing: it was passionate talk and again I was furious with the self-pity which so diminished me and the self, self, self which was—literally, it seemed now—consuming me. I, too had wanted to be a preacher, a Bunyan, a Wesley, a man with a message and a purpose and a vision. And here I stood, behind the shoulder of one who had: and even while he spoke, even though I was wanting to be filled with his words, I could not keep off my own despair.

Sometimes it is hard to hold onto the idea that it is the quality of the observer that matters and not the material which makes up the experience. I know, or I believe, or I hope that a description of what happened to me, if well done, has no less validity than a description of what had happened to him. But his stories of fights with the police, acting improvised plays in Harlem, arranging 'happenings' in Central Park, debating with the students at Columbia, running news sheets which were 'busted' by agents of the F.B.I. and making underground films which were banned by everybody under the sun—it *does* appear more exciting than my affairs. The black American spreading the words and capturing the audience; the diffident Englishman silently at his elbow, falling apart.

Yet they were not fools who came to Rod's parties. Having given the floor to the actor for a considerable time, two hard-headed English liberals, academics, serious-faced and very patient, began to take his arguments apart. What did he *mean* by saying that every black man should know how to make a Molotov cocktail? Was he *serious?* What did he *mean* by saying that America was a Fascist State? Fascist like Germany in 1943, in 1938, in 1936 or in 1932—when? What did he mean by the 'tyranny of free institutions'? There was some confusion there. He was no match for them. In their own way they were merciless and bullying and only when he had been forced to a description of what his own situation—as a black actor trying to get work in the film business—what that had been like and still *was* like (he claimed) though in different offices and different words, only then did they relent. I was relieved that the messianic part had been stripped away. I had believed in him when he spoke: now I saw that it was too easy to call on the devil and all his works. For some related reason I was less uneasy about my own troubles; less ashamed of their smallness. In fact I wish I could have proposed them to those two hard heads and they would have given me the benefit of the intelligently summarized liberal views which would have helped; though perhaps they would not have been as certain as they were about politics and society. No one is, about people and their individual reactions, their private thoughts and personal relationships: there are no boundaries, few essential markers, a scarcity of apt comparisons—which is why, I suppose, any news from the interior of a mind is welcome news, even good news, and as such can take its place as being of general value even as much as news of important external worlds. But it was unlike me to be so much in favour of a man one minute and so against him the next: to be unable myself to see the faults in his argument and then to be unable to see any virtue in it. There was a total loss of centre—for now I *can* see his virtue; arguments are something else.

I could go on around the party but I am as hesitant to do that now as I was hesitant to leave then. I feel you know enough about it. An interesting minor irony was that, as it was my ambition to say nothing (indeed I was almost hoarse and used the defect to help me out). So I found myself in the company of people who would have frightened me off at other times: a keen listener is always welcome I suppose. People began to go about half-past one. At about three o'clock there were less than a dozen of us left: Jane, Rod's girl-friend, made some coffee. I put brandy in mine but was either in a state of controlled drunkenness or beyond it, I don't know: I was immensely tired, I was deeply and violently tired and the slightest exertion—even going across to pour that brandy into my coffee, set my heart jumping, my blood fiercely rushing through veins which seemed to have become fine fibres rubbed the wrong way by the coursing of this trapped and frightened flood. I have given you enough images of my 'mind': it was, by now, like one of those neat and well-protected, well-planned and hygienic little fortress towns, self-sufficient and imperturbable, which suddenly finds itself bombed, shelled, burnt and brutalized and, at the end of the day, deserted by all but those who could not leave and had no means or no alternative.

Rod saw me to the door and said I looked a damned sight better than when I'd arrived, asked me when I was going 'up home' again and was wanly friendly.

The 'tough' was still at the top of my street. I saw him in the doorway of the tobacconist's shop: his white shirt must have been of an odd material because it glowed in the dark. I was ready for him. I wanted him. I clenched

171

and unclenched my fists—so far away, those hands, such strange objects, fingers, those joints, the slippery nails, the awkward thumb—did it go inside the fist or outside the fist? I'd forgotten if I ever knew. I tried it first one way and then the other as I walked towards him. Clenching and unclenching. Neither seemed right; neither seemed comfortable.

I remembered my father and the way he used to work in the fields on the farm the days my mother let him take me. I saw him working, never stopping it seemed, and myself as feeble as a kitten. I had my father's build. I pulled back my shoulders; I strutted a little: probably I swayed, drunkenly. I went right up to him and put up my fists—still uncertain about the thumbs. The street was deserted but for us—eerie, lovely and peaceful it looked: the wind soft in the trees, the air warm and fresh—and there, Tagon Street—where was my nightmare? Some of the houses being 'done up', some already painted white, window boxes and shrubs, trees at the bottom of it and handsome cars like decorations along the kerbs—where was the fear in it? Where the monsters? It was a lovely street, masculine, unpretentious, much better than Rod's street, I thought happily, full of differences and possibilities unlike that pat little estate agents' dream of his—yes, a good choice, Tagon Street, a real place.

Perhaps not all of that settled summary came to mind as I squared up in front of the tired, unsmiling young man who had waited for so long, but some of it was certainly there: something of a farewell about it. I thought he would flatten me and was urged on by that. It would be a final blow I'd give much to receive.

I waved my fists but he did not budge. 'Come on then,' I said or muttered—did not shout, conscious of the peace and people sleeping. 'Come on then, let's get it over with. You've been asking for it all day. Eh? Eh?'

He spoke in the same flat voice he'd used in the morning: but all belligerence was gone, all swagger drained away. The tone was miserable and hopeless.

'Where is she? She isn't with you, is she? I know that —I'm not asking you that. She out wid another bloke? That's all you need tell us, mister. She got a reg'lar, steady bloke?'

I dropped my fists: my self-pity heaved into him and I wanted to lie to ease his suffering.

'I think she . . . she has . . . yes . . . I think so. Somebody'—to help; would it help? 'Somebody she's known all her life.'

'A childhood sweetheart?'

'That's it. That's right. Childhood sweethearts. That's what she said.' I paused. 'You can't win against *them*,' I said. 'Not against childhood things.'

He nodded and went away, still his hands in his pockets, still the jaunty walk, still the shirt collar carefully over the jacket's collar, his feet loud and clear on the pavement. Down the lighted way towards black London. Before he'd turned to go I'd seen such hopelessness as must have been in part a reflection of my own. And as I trailed down the street, the pain which had been staved off by the intervention of the party returned with fullest force.

I thought I was dying. My chest was pierced by a single sharp pain which seemed to come in at my back and be aimed at my heart; my legs were weak; my head was ill; I panted for breath—and when that terrible vision of the raw unskinned screaming child came once again into my throat and once again kicked and screamed in my throat, then I knew I wanted to do one thing only before it was all over. One single thing.

I packed my bag: I endured the time until morning by taking two more sleeping pills and sipping from the glass of brandy which Geoffrey had left for me. Just after eight I went out to look for a taxi and went to Euston

173

There I had to wait three hours for a train to Cumberland. I sat on a bench, unmoving, utterly convinced that I would die soon and would have welcomed it, wanting to be relieved of this burden of a body, wanting to be free from the dangers which this ejection into a new world had brought on me, wanting to die; in so far as I am honest, honestly wanting to live no more after one last act.

9

On the train I sat by the window and watched the country glide past me, framed and silent; the train's noise blotted out other sounds. I was soon wet with perspiration but did not even take off my jacket. I was too upset to want to eat though I bought a cup of coffee when the man came around from the buffet. I did not try to read. I held myself against the pains and assaults which now beat against me without any pause and I used the damaged eye as a connection with myself, squeezing it and fingering it, cultivating its soreness.

'I cannot paint what then I was.' Wordsworth, in *Tintern Abbey,* writes that he cannot describe the raptures and ecstasies of himself as a boy alone in Nature; and it is possible to associate with that, to remember times of such mind-blown pleasure and be unable to do more than imagine you feel them; or remember the consequences of the feeling. As I write now, I have lost much of the memory of the feeling of that journey: or I have suppressed it. I need to be without it to go on now —there are things you cannot hold in memory without their force fixing you in their grip. I would suggest, however, that what I felt then was the reverse of what Wordsworth described; that all those happy and positive forces which swept through him, the light and sun and laughter of it, was turned to darkness, to misery, to a force of unhappiness constantly beating and crunching the brain. For it seemed that inside the skull was some membrane of self-consciousness holding the brain in place and it was as if cramp had gripped that and seized it, somehow drying it slowly all that day, so slowly that the movement was hardly observable, and threatened to last forever before reaching its end; I was that skull, cramping, crushed, I splitting, I ripping the membrane.

We arrived in Carlisle when it was still afternoon and when I got to her house in my own town it was a balmy evening—sweet smells, peace, warm air, soothing light, open spaces— and the white houses on the council estate looked so comfortable, the gardens so trim, lately planted trees beginning to grow up along the kerbside; what often seemed a desolate place—this well-planned council estate removed from the centre of the town and left pub-less and shop-less—now looked like a calm, established suburb.

It is difficult to be inconspicuous in any small residential district but particularly, perhaps, in a working-class street or a working-class estate. There are few points of general interest, there are virtually no places to visit except a particular house: and I wanted to keep her house in view.

My plan was simple. I would follow her: I would talk to her; and we would go on from there. I did not know what I would say or what I would do. In my fantasies we ran away to Scotland; we met daily and walked; we lived together and I looked after her. I was sure that the solution would present itself once I'd made contact. I was of course prepared to be rebuffed: or I am sure that I was not so utterly stupid as not to have been so prepared: but I did not seriously consider it.

I saw Lizzie's husband come out just before seven in charcoal-grey suit, white shirt, the collar tucked over the jacket—almost certainly on his way to the pub. It was still daylight and I thought back to the long light evenings when I would walk through the fields in daylight after ten o'clock—northern nights, cool but not chill with clouds motionless in the sky—waiting for dawn. I walked along the Avenue and back again. I could wait: I had nothing else to do. I glanced at my watch from time to time and tapped my foot as if impatient. Watchers would be bound to think I was being stood up by some girl, I thought.

A gang of small boys was playing football on a triangular patch of green in the middle of which was a lamp post. Husbands were tending gardens: from open windows came the sound of Anglican hymns—the Sunday service on television. I remembered the hymns and was afraid to cry once more.

The dark glasses made me more conspicuous than I wished but my swollen eye would have been even more singular. I tried, by ostentatious attention with a fluttered handkerchief, to convey to the invisible observers that the sunglasses were not an affectation but a necessity. I walked down the Avenue again.

I'd seen Lizzie often over the last twelve years; about the town. She had not 'gone to pieces': I never saw her with her hair wound in curlers and stuffed under the bandage of a scarf; her figure thickened a little but very little. Her husband had a good job and she herself worked: she dressed well. She had three children: two sons by him and my daughter. I'd kept track of my daughter; my flesh: it would have been hard not to in that small place. I'd never made myself known to her of course nor even been as 'obvious' as I was being now, coming to the estate: I'd never hung around her nor had I in any way spied on her. I had kept out of her life. She is called Tracy.

To see her gave me such a blow of pleasure, regrets, pride; some such inextricable mixture—such sweet, heavy blows, that I could have taken forever. She looked like my mother, I thought. Same chin, same clench of eyes, same skin and hair.

I just wanted to speak to her. I had come three hundred miles that day to speak to her. I have relived that insane day in some measure for her: in some place my reliving it has expiated what I might have done to her; as it has come into existence because of her: I write out of her and for her.

She was with a friend: they might have been twins by their dress. Bottle-green school blazers over flimsy blouses: knee-length white socks, brown sandals and extremely short tartan skirts: I considered them to be far too short. They passed me on the other side of the Avenue and went into Tracy's house.

Waiting now ought to have been unnerving but I was so beset and beleaguered in my mind that I did not get particularly anxious. I had all the time in the world: the longer I waited, the better, for after I had spoken to her—what then? I knew that the likeliest conclusion would be none at all; and I was threatening myself with this death. I can only write about it so tentatively now that it almost rings false; as over-caution may take on the character of cowardice. To talk of thoughts and death when someone is really dying: to talk of love for an unknown daughter when a mother known and better known daily, hourly loved and loving; to remember such mean and unhappy, such ignoble and miserable times when what I have now is none of these. Why? And again I must say there is no other way: this fiction is the only way to tell that story and I need to tell the story in much the same way and with much the same force as I needed to talk to my daughter on that docile Sunday evening. Perhaps I thought that she would dissolve the child which threatened to choke me; or let it come out and grow.

I imagine that she had come home at 'seven o'clock as promised' and was now begging for an extension. She was only twelve even though her way of dress being adopted by anyone between twelve and twenty, her 'little girl' look, rather perversely, made her look older: but she was twelve and this was no Gomorrah.

They came out, the two of them, walking rapidly, quickly putting a safe distance between themselves and the house. I followed them.

The plan collapsed the instant I began to execute it. I could not upset her by imposing on her in any way: though I had sent her into the world, in the world's terms I had no connection with her and there was no way in which I could establish one without bringing her some pain or embarrassment. I walked behind them —about twenty yards behind them; they were heading for the centre of the town and so was I. I slowed down so as not to be 'following', but they must have lost their initial urgency, for the distance between us did not increase. I saw myself trailing behind the two young girls, their heads practically joined together as they whispered and giggled with each other, their arms linked, four thin white-socked legs clicking away—I saw myself as one of those doleful heroes in some Continental film: very clearly I 'saw' a melancholy figure who might have been played by Marcello Mastroianni, glumly trailing after his 'daughter', casting sorrowful glances in the general direction of the camera and eventually drifting off to look at the sea and light a cigarette. End titles. And for a few moments I 'played' that scene and was pleased to play it, pleased to do anything to keep my thoughts off the pain. I loved her very much, I thought. . . .

As my daughter had drawn me away from London, giving me a reason and an objective—possibly the only one which could have taken me from what was closing in on me—so now she towed me into the town. I wanted to sleep. I wanted to sleep for as long as I could.

It would be poignant to report an incident, however minor, say that the girls mistook me for a would-be boy friend, or a threat—suspicious. She could have 'recognized' something in me which was her and somehow been drawn to do something out of character which

179

would have been a signal to me. They could have teased me along, the pair of them, deciding I was a harmless fool, and led me around the loops of alleyways in the town until they came to the boys they were undoubtedly preparing themselves for.

Nothing happened. We arrived in the centre of the town and they went into a coffee bar and I went into a pub. I drank moderately: I spoke to nobody. There were one or two came in that I knew but none well enough to intrude on the privacy I drew around myself. And I knew them only slightly: I've lost the few friends I had in the town; they've moved or changed and, twelve years away from it, together with the fact that I never belonged to a gang or a clique as a youth, means that now I have about the same contacts as a fairly regular tourist. I drank moderately and in the friendly place, being so tired I was almost in a swoon with it: I drifted over the previous day; my mind seemed to free itself and float up and slowly turn back the spool and linger over the sequences of that previous day. It was then I decided I would try to write it down—would seriously do so. I had kept this as a thread during that day, as if by following it I would find my way out of the labyrinth; but I had never been settled enough to begin to employ it. Now I saw it was a real alternative, and a solution—possibly the only one.

Tired, tired. Music from a tape-recorder: muzak from discreet speakers. Strings and melody; nothing harsh, nothing strained. Moderate. I would be moderate; I would practise understatement: I would say, 'Nothing, really: a sort of psychological migraine—a couple of metaphorical codeines and we'll be right as rain.' Breakdown? Breakthrough? 'Take it easy on yourself,' they say. I cannot paint what then I was. A few broken images. Coleridge stoned and friends fighting for a state pension for him. Who hung the Albatross *here*? 'Maybe baby, if I had you-u-u. Maybe baby. . . .' The froth on the beer thinned out and I looked through the beer and the glass to my hands cupped underneath. Sea air sours it, so they say. Be moderate in all things. Respect the Golden Mean. Ignore the Golden Calf. Take care not to be fooled by those hectic enthusiasms which spend passion so extravagently: they will bankrupt. Do not be influenced by those who say 'The End is near, the Apocalypse is upon us, the worst of times is coming': the worst of times was always coming. It has come and there was a Flood that was an End, they thought: but it seems it only cleared the ground for new beginnings. Despise excess: be immoderate only in that. Tired? *Rather* tired.

I went out and it was still light: they had the street lights on but they were forlorn; the street was not full but there were sufficient people here to give it some slight feeling of Promenade. I was surprised to find that I was quite drunk.

When I saw my mother's house I had no will left. I had not the strength to take on her care for me. I went past it and along the backs of the terrace until I came to ours: opposite the backyard was our allotment and the shed. I went in it and lay down to sleep.

It was uncomfortable. As quietly as I could I rearranged things to give myself some space. By the time I had done this I was in a state of exhausted exasperation and I knew that I had to sleep. I could see another avalanche of fear slipping at the top of my mind, stirring, shuddering, preparing to crash down into it. I could not take any more.

There was nothing to drink so I had to chew the sleeping pills: I ate five, to be quite certain and also to give myself an even chance of not waking at all.

*　　*　　*　　*

It was not 'all over'.

My father 'found' me: he speaks of it with pride as if he'd gone on a treasure hunt and got first prize. In hospital I was kept under observation for a few days and then I came here, to this house. For about a month the storms in my head were much as they had been on that Saturday. My mother cooked for me and left me a cold lunch when she went out to work. I told her that my term did not start until October: and then I told her I was writing a book and had been given a sabbatical term to do it in. She accepted the lies without question and looked after me carefully. I did not try to take my own life but was often totally convinced that I would die. I lived from moment to moment, went out only for short strolls in broad daylight, listened to music on the wireless, read poetry. I found that poetry was the only material I could endure. I learnt a great many poems by heart—at one stage I used to get myself through the day by setting myself the target of learning one poem by heart: *and* remembering what I had learnt on the previous days. I used the Oxford Book of English Verse and at one time knew more than fifty of the poems by heart: I couldn't recite you one, now. I had other methods for passing the day.

There had been a psychiatrist at the hospital who'd said 'to drop in and see him if I wanted help'. I did. I arrived at the hospital on a wintry day, muffled up with coat and scarf and gloves. He suggested Prospect Sanatorium as a voluntary patient for a few weeks. I went there.

As soon as I got there I knew I had to keep hold of my normal life as hard as I could. I could have spent years in the place 'exploring my personality' and I would have enjoyed it but the risk was too great. I have not that much time or courage. I wanted to find the means to contain what had happened to me and to build up a new life: it had to be a new life.

I took up supply-teaching, part time. The money, of

course, was necessary (though my mother would have kept me), but I wanted to keep in the world. I went back at Christmas for a fortnight and then decided to live out in the winter in Cumberland. Again I taught and once again my mother and I compared school notes in the evenings. I was not strong enough to go back to London, not on the terms I wanted. A few letters to the college from myself and various doctors regularized the position there: the job will be available to me again in September.

Now it is June. I will never be 'cured' in the sense of regaining the personality I once had: but I would consider such a cure to be a failure. What I had I do not want: I would rather live less securely than live as falsely as that: rather, indeed, be foolish than resort to past certainties. That is one of the things I find about trying to live in what I want to be my own way: I do extremely stupid things—make what are virtually confessions to someone who is not much more than an acquaintance: boast of future plans, several ambitions which I do not, truly, hold but somehow I want to hear myself say it all—perhaps to display openly how stupid it is: use my stupidity as a midwife to greater and lesser inanities: or to a new peace.

Sometimes I see myself back in that room in Tagon Street. It is again that Saturday and again I am woken up by the dust-cart. But I am not startled. My eye is swollen, but I am not alarmed. I am in no danger. I lie back and stretch and relax—because it is Saturday morning and there is no rush to do anything. And I think that all that I have written is a nightmare, an hallucination, the counter-image of my solid self there, easy in the soft bed.

More often I see myself walking down the street as I will when I do return, which I will. And I hope that I will no longer cramp myself into the postures of defeat. I want to be as happy as I possibly can be: I want to sink what I have in order to find what I may be capable of: I no longer want to accept the pact, the bargain, the treaty made between myself and my past. I am sick of the past. I want to spend my life being more and more what I am—following fantasies, realizing dreams.

In a few minutes I shall go in to see my mother and read to her some more Jane Austen, whose genius and qualities are so far from my own ambition that once I would have cringed and thought less of myself for not being capable of that view of life. Now there must be no cringing and no regrets: richer and poorer, better and worse, sickness and health—yes—but no fear, no aping, no shame at your own way.

Finding the way—the salvationist ring is justified. If we do not accept a way, we must find one: even if we think we drift, to drift you need to be moved and sustained by a current, a hidden way: the way is the truth and finding the truth takes the life.

At three-thirty I take her tea and a sandwich. I follow the meal-schedule of the sanatorium. She will sip an inch of tea and, to please me, take a minute bite from a sandwich. She will say I look tired and should not work so hard: she knows I have been trying to finish this book today and she is concerned that it should not exhaust me. She has never talked to me about those bad months, the hospital, the clinic, the silences. The house is quiet about us.

10

I saw Rod again recently, while I was writing that last chapter. He was up here on a visit and, as always on these well-spaced, carefully ordered returns, there was a sufficient reason for him to be interviewed on 'Cumbrian' television. A collection of his short stories was about to be published—*Our Lot* was the title, though none of the stories was called by that name. The local television company never liked to admit that they wanted to interview him merely because of his own television work (particularly as he operates on a different channel) and the stories gave them an entrée on their own terms; as he realized. Moreover, they could have some fun attempting to rile him on the 'local boy made good' line, which was invariably discomfiting; Rod realized that, too. Finally, they liked him along for the London gossip he brought; they would pump him about television politics as exiled courtiers must once have been avid for news from the palace—'who's in, who's out, who's up, who's down'; and Rod realized that, too.

He enjoyed being interviewed.

My mother called me down to see it. She used to get up in the late afternoon and watch television for an hour or so, never missing the local news and magazine. It must have been an effort for her to get out of the chair and come to the bottom of the stairs but she was pleased to see someone she knew on the screen and wanted me to share the pleasure. I was reading in my bedroom and came down only out of regard for her feelings, I thought. I arrived near the end.

He was in big close-up and looked very well. Would he ever think of coming to live in Cumberland permanently? Well, he often thought about it, but the difficulty was to find a job. You fellas from down South came up and pinched all the decent jobs. It was trouble enough for local people to park here once they'd left, never mind live here: and the time wasn't far off when you'd need a passport to cross Shap Fell. Seriously though, to quote a mutual acquaintance, the thing was to live in one place or another. It was no good having a toe-hold in a place. Better to get out and come back as a visitor until the day you came back for good. Besides, it could be a strain—you forgot so many details, who was married and who'd had twins, who'd died and who'd gone to Australia.... There was some talk, said the interviewer, of a film being made in Cumberland based on one of his books—any comment? None; said Rod.... After the rather awkward hiatus, a last question. Why the title—*Our Lot*. It means my generation and my birthplace, said Rod, there are stories set in London and here, in Cumberland. It could also mean our destiny or fate especially as in *that* context 'lot' has a colloquial air which is ironical about its own meaning. That takes some swallowing, said the interviewer, and thank you. Thank *you*, said Rod, all you need is a good digestion and you might say, plenty of guts.

There followed a film on lambing.

My mother had been delighted, in a quiet way, until the very last word. 'Guts' was a coarse word and people who had been educated ought to be able to avoid it. I had seen her flinch—or perhaps, knowing she would, I had imagined it. But I knew I had imagined her reaction correctly. Poor sweetheart, she had no flesh between her sense of what was right and her contact with the world. Yet there was some change in her not giving way to a positive comment

'What did you think of the interview?' I asked, when

the programme was done. She had asked me to turn off the television; her eyes tired quickly.

'Very nice.' She was cautious, scenting I was teasing her out.

'He's pleasant, isn't he?'

'He has a nice smile; yes.'

'Come on, mother, he charms you, doesn't he? All the nice old ladies like him.'

'More than you do.'

'What makes you say that?'

'I can tell.' She was pleased to rest on her certainty: yet it moved me, now, that she should feel her understanding of me to be such a comfort.

'What do you mean?' I persisted; I had got rid of that binding question over the past few years—but in this time together, old connections had been re-established. 'Come on you old teaser—why do you say I don't like Rod?'

'I didn't say that.' But fearing her scrupulous pedantry might break the thread, she added, 'Something like it I did say, though.'

'You didn't like the word "guts", did you?'

'No. I didn't like that.' She hesitated: I was willing her to add the next observation: 'I thought he let himself down there.'

'I knew you would!' I smiled at her and suddenly felt so elated that I went across to her and kissed her brow. 'You silly old Scot—you really are a dour piece of work, aren't you, eh?' Again I kissed her, moved by the shyness of her smile, the appreciation of such recognition tempered by anxiety at the proximity of flattery. 'Did Rabbie Burns not leave his traces in your part of the Lowlands, eh?'

'Away with you. There's been far too much said against that poor man. We don't *know* what he was like and so there's no sense in guesswork.'

I had not put on the light and the twilight gently

entered, softening the room, the neat, bright furnishings, the shine and glitter of it all. There was a coal fire despite the mild weather; she needed it. She had a rug over her knees and sat very upright in the chair, as unafraid of her death as it is possible to appear. I sat down beside her and took her arm.

'I'm sorry you have the impression I don't like Rod,' I said, glad to see on the surface something which had been nudging it for a long time.

'It's all right, my dear.' She patted my hand.

'I think he said "guts" because he was nervous." I spoke deliberately—borrowing her pace—determined to exonerate him from her unfair charge. 'He'd probably given away more than he wanted to when he talked about destiny and fate—those are the sort of notions you want to keep to yourself. And in a way, it was nice of him to be so honest in his answer. But when the interviewer made a joke of it he regretted it: and then the only thing he could do was to annul it by capping the interviewer's remark. But because he was nervous and because there was so little time, he couldn't think of anything particularly witty and so the best he could do was to play around with the word—"eat?"— swallow? *Swallow:* That was it. And besides wanting to do that, he wanted to get one in at the interviewer for "exposing" him *and* justify himself some way : so "guts" suggested that the interviewer might be lacking them and that he himself had them. It could also, for some people, be thought of as a decent come-back. Dad, if he's seen it down in the pub, he'll be spouting it without fail, convinced that somehow Rod showed all sorts of likeable qualities by saying "guts". Don't wince, mother. It's not a swear word.'

'You certainly explain him in detail.'

'Well, I think it's Rod who has the guts in these situations. It isn't easy to be on parade all the time.'

'He chose the life,' she said, carefully, 'he must have known what it would lead to.'

'Nobody can know what such a choice will lead to, mother.'

'They must accept the consequences, however, once the choice is made.'

'It is possible to make a bad choice and recognize it and change. Or who would ever be able to leave a life of sin, eh? Mistress Severity.'

'Maybe.' She held my hand most tenderly. 'I'm glad you're here—with me.'

'I'm glad to be here.'

The rush of grief came to my throat but I checked it, forced it back. She did not need my tears.

When the knock came at the door I was convinced it was Rod. There had been two letters from him—cheerful, decent letters: I had replied to the first—a note of acknowledgment. The second needed no such seal. There was patronage in the letters, true, but a generous feeling, too: for he must have known how I was likely to receive his interest and yet he had not let that stop him showing it.

I put on the light at the door and waited a moment, despite the second more impatient knock until my mother's eyes had grown used to the light and she had tidied up the rug as she would want it.

It was the doctor.

I went upstairs while he examined her. There, following my line of thought, I looked up what I had written about Rod and found that almost the last remark I made about him was that he was 'wanly friendly'. Which was accurate. But if Rod had walked in to this house, I would have welcomed him.

'That's big of you!' I could hear him saying, mocking mock gratitude. 'Thank you *very* much, Ted, and excuse me while I wipe away a tear.' But he would be friendly about it and even pleased, I knew that now.

The doctor left without coming up to see me. That meant there was no material change in her condition. I gave her a few minutes to herself and went across to my window, knocking off the light so that I could look over the rooftops, unseen.

A half moon was hardening into light. I thought of the fells around the sanatorium, how the moonlight had made such a beauty and a mystery of them. And of Tagon Street where street lamps overlaid its effect. The doctor's car jumped into life and the noise flicked my nerves. I would have liked to follow him out, to go and be useful in the world and active.

'Edward. Edward.' Her voice was neither anxious nor self-pitying.

I went down to her.